T0208580

Out of the Shadows

The Ancient Ones

Sharon Riegie Maynard

iUniverse, Inc.
New York   Bloomington

Out of the Shadows
The Ancient Ones

This is a work of fiction. All of the characters, names, incidents, organizations, and dialogue in this novel are either the products of the author's imagination or are used fictitiously.

iUniverse books may be ordered through booksellers or by contacting:

iUniverse
1663 Liberty Drive
Bloomington, IN 47403
www.iuniverse.com
1-800-Authors (1-800-288-4677)

Because of the dynamic nature of the Internet, any Web addresses or links contained in this book may have changed since publication and may no longer be valid. The views expressed in this work are solely those of the author and do not necessarily reflect the views of the publisher, and the publisher hereby disclaims any responsibility for them.

ISBN: 978-1-4401-4441-7 (sc)
ISBN: 978-1-4401-4440-0 (ebk)

Printed in the United States of America

iUniverse rev. date: 7/3/2009

For my children, my treasures and most wonderful teachers,
Elizabeth, Teresa, Jennifer, Michelle, Aondrea, Diana, Donald,
Carolyn and David.
Noel and Keith

And my grandchildren through whom the joy of life continues,
Sara, Alex, Alyssa, and Anais

My deepest thanks to Connie, who saw the mission of this book
and made its initial publication possible and my many students who
caused my questions and made this publication possible.

"A bird does not sing because it has an answer,
It sings because it has a song."

Unknown

Shadows

Earth whirled. A blue-green sphere in the spectrum of space, a planet critical in a desperate plan for survival. Life was being sucked from every family member. A parasitic force lay hidden and deadly amongst its host. In this new world where energy became solid, individuals would have to face the truth. Evil swirled among them. Indeed, it owned them.

The possibility of breaking free brought a degree of hope. Thrilled at the opportunity, millions had volunteered to participate in the Earth mission. The first step was to make the planet inhabitable and the second was to identify and break free of the evil.

Energy swirled as songs, dances and prayers broadcast the vision. Then a beautiful new planet came forth out of the mists

This new planet was watched, adjusted until it was ready to sustain life. Then those chosen for the mission were sent onto the planet. Their energy bodies were protected and provided movement within physical vehicles. Patterns for these body suit vehicles had been made with much attention to detail. Two separate body suits, a key factor for success. In addition to the codes for the mission, it contained codes for returning Home and circuitries to communication centers off of the planet.

The dream of glorious creations became real soon after the planet's manifestation. As the Ancient Ones explored the surface of their new home, they made contact with the Earth's stored resources and brought forth abundant food, lush gardens, fragrant flowers, and amazing animal life.

But, shortly after the second stage of the plan was initiated, the parasitic Outsiders discovered their intent. The Outsiders accessed the body suit pattern, re-engineered the circuitry, crashed the evolutionary path, and re-routed communication through their own systems. All of these changes created greater fear and ongoing subjugation within the Ancient Ones.

Soon after the step to identify the Outside parasites was discovered, all who had volunteered for the mission and those who came to help were birthed into crippled body vehicles. False systems emerged that clouded the original plans and the great hope of the Galactic family for freedom was lost in the shadows of survival. What had been possible became only a memory.

The Mission
Remembered

As quickly as sound, Myra sped from the brilliance of her home. With a firm grasp of her vibrational chart, she maneuvered through the approaching waves of darkness into the magnetic fields surrounding her target. Moving with precision and grace, she came to hover in a small, sparse room. She slipped through the form of a woman large with child and into the tiny physical body suit.

With a sense of triumph and excitement, Myra stretched her self to explore all areas of the suit, the vehicle that would give her weight and presence on this new planet. She listened to the beat of the heart, monitored the breathing mechanism and marveled at the perfection. As she settled in, Myra remembered its small quarters and smiled.

Feeling the effects of her travel, Myra shut down her thoughts to doze, slightly aware of the whirring and humming of this suit. There are some things I'll have to get used to she decided as sleep overcame her.

Muffled shouts shook Myra awake. Waves of pain rippled through her space. The rhythm of the heart and the breathing apparatus changed. She felt sensations that were foreign to her. Unfamiliar sounds, harsh and loud, penetrated her enclosed space.

Mentally, Myra quickly moved to switch on her communication systems. Why hadn't she done that before?

Her space was being jostled, falling and moving. It was difficult to turn on the switches to activate the codes to her outreach systems with this terror and the jerky movements. Myra calmed herself and commanded the body suit to quiet, to slow. With great effort Myra created distance from the harshness and confusion to allow herself to locate the switches. With focus she pulled them as she had practiced so many times.

Nothing.

Not possible she thought. She breathed, remembered and tried again.

Nothing.

Her energy slowed… stopped … started again. Even as her carrying space quieted Myra's fear escalated. She searched the body's circuitry. Again she reached out- nothing. She scanned the vehicle. There were missing systems, incorrect codes. What had happened? Control center, the channel for her team was weak, so weak that she could barely hear their voices. There were major problems and Myra had no way to contact her team. The assurance of Self, of purpose, of mission began to fade.

Now Myra screamed. Help! Something is wrong with me! I'm not okay, I'm lost! I'll never make it.

Then came the shadows.

Eve wandered down the sandy path toward the home she shared with Adam. Eve smiled as she watched her songs add color to the garden and observed as her dance called to birds flying through the trees. Amazing adventure.

She had spent the day with an Ancient teacher who had approached her shortly after sunrise.

"Come," she had invited, "we need you now."

Eve's heart sang with the opportunity. She had not conceived that there could be such joy.

Very precisely her teacher had explained and reminded her of the composition of the energy fields around the planet. In her initial task of calling forth resources and beauty from the Earth Mother, Eve had forgotten that the energies from outside societies had been carried onto this new home with Adam. Those parasitic energies would continue to pollute and kill as long as they remained hidden, unseen. The law of manifestation was causing all energies to appear: love, fear and the evil of parasitics, just as had been planned. Today her teacher had reminded her of the true purpose of the law of manifestation, to make evil visible.

She and Adam had spent a great deal of time exploring this new home, he holding the remembrance of all that was possible and the focus of love. She working directly with the Mother Earth to assure that this planet could sustain their life with abundance and ease. They had thought that they were ready to begin the preparation to bring more of the volunteers onto this new home.

Because of today's lesson, Eve realized there was another step. First she must discern the energy of Divine Good and of Parasitic Evil. She had been reminded of the necessity of that part of the female mission. Unless she focused to discern the quality of manifested forms, the evil of the Outsiders would take away the vibrancy and life of the volunteers. With the help of her Ancient teacher, today Eve was able to taste and know the difference between good and evil forms.

Her soul sang in ways she had never imagined possible

CHAPTER 1

Passionate crowds roamed the streets of Tyree. The city's instability had brought the government's policies into question and citizens with a range of opinions clashed and fought. Mobs ruled the outlying districts with no thought of penance. This afternoon was moderately calm. The Rycur, policing authorities of the Tyreans, filled the area as the Greater Council met to debate and decide possible solutions.

Since early in Earth's history there had been recurring cycles of imbalance. Periods of stable growth were followed by major downfalls into conflict, fear, and anger. The eruptions would demolish much of what had been accomplished. This fall created vulnerability that affected everyone including societies in close proximity to the Earth.

Myra stood behind the grandiose columns of the great Earth Council Hall, Tuma's arm around her. In all of Earth's history there had not been a more momentous time and this day was the pinnacle. She regarded the scene before her. Every particle of her light body was alert as Myra stood silently sipping her beverage. As a guest from the world region seven klicons from their home star, Myra had come often to help balance the energy fields. The current mission had included another agenda, to remind those on the Earth of their original plan. This plan had been long forgotten and hidden in the shadows of corruption. Today those on the Gegfad mission had proposed to the Council that they be allowed to extend their visit and begin teaching the citizens of Tyree. Those whose vested interest was in power and control were outraged and had incited riots.

Suddenly shouts followed by loud clashes came from the street a stone's throw from the Court area. A small group at the edge of the Court's garden hurled rocks into the crowd and then scurried into the safety of a small enclosure of trees.

Myra moved closer to Tuma as they watched the police converge on the crowd in the streets. With clubs and swords they were forcing them to break up. Protesting citizens fled into the alleyways.

Emotions had even erupted amongst the Council during the discussions. Anxiety filled the air of the Council enclosure. Myra reacted to the disruptive energies, the whispered tones, animated gestures and sober faces by moving closer to Tuma. She closed her eyes and silently transformed the heaviness around her.

Unlike the Tryrean's desensitized bodies, the vibrations of the light bodies on the Gegfad mission were keen. They felt the subtlest energy disruption. The essence from Home flowed through each of them. It carried information and a sense of love that kept them connected and stable. Because of the artificial systems within the Earth citizens, their energy flow from Home was limited and disjointed. It was one reason for the recurring imbalance. With the uninterrupted flow between those on mission, what one experienced, all experienced, what enriched one was enriching to all. It created a strong sense of Oneness. Myra knew that it was critical to the Gegfad team that any hint of the heavy, negative energy be quickly cleared from their fields. Otherwise, Earth's energy density would cover their subtle vibrational breath and endanger them as it had the Earth's.

Myra turned to Tuma. He was scanning the garden and the streets, occasionally looking at the doors of the Council Hall. When he sensed her watching him, he turned and smiled.

"I am thinking about the excitement we had about this planet," she said softly. "Do you remember how carefully the Galactic Council considered ideas to get our family out from under the parasitic ownership?"

Tuma nodded.

"How ironic is it that here we are still facing the same situation. We are still trapped by Outsiders committed to usury, greed and power regardless of it's cost to our family."

"Ironic and sad," Tuma replied. "Just imagine where our family would be now if our plan had succeeded. If our first families had been able to identify and remove the parasitics with just a command, simply by the right to command." Tuma shook his head. "It was a magnificent plan."

"Well, this would not be happening," Myra said, gesturing to the streets.

"Nor would this debate," added Tuma. "How can we hope to awaken the consciousness of our family while they are trapped in body suits crippled by the parasitic Outsiders? No one knows what level of awareness is needed to counteract the re-engineered systems or if it is even possible."

Sensing his weariness, Myra stepped closer to gather his hands in hers and shift the energy.

CHAPTER 2

Myra heard voices coming from the streets. Far away at first, the sounds came closer until she could hear chants louder and louder, "Send them home, send them home, send them home." A few within Council moved together as if in agreement to the chant and turned to look toward the various groups of those on mission, including Tuma and Myra.

She turned toward the sound and the back of her neck prickled. Tuma moved to stand between her and the crowd, pulling her close. Myra shuddered.

He closed his eyes, moved his attention to a central place in his mind and blocked the heavy vibrations. Myra felt the energy lessening and glanced up into Tuma's eyes. How she loved him! Together they dissolved the frequencies before they could impact the energy fields of their group.

Tuma kissed the top of her head but they both sensed the growing restlessness. Myra scanned those on the streets. Their fists were raised as they shouted and shoved others who seemed to disagree. She noticed one young man. He stood out, blond, taller than most. He moved with the agility of a cat, in one group one minute and quickly shifting to incite another group the next. He seemed to be purposely weaving through the crowds fermenting conflict, not conflict directed at himself but between others. And he often pointed out the groups of guests Myra realized, pointed at them, at Tuma and at her.

Myra was not surprised but intrigued. Often those who worked to keep the citizens angry and fearful did their work in secret. Here was one in the light of day, one she could observe with different eyes. So she closed her eyes and shifted to her etheric vision and looked out over the crowds. There they were-the Outsiders. Unseen by the citizens of Tyree, indeed all Earth inhabitants, they became clearly visible in her sight. They had so invaded the space around this young man that they were directing his actions, speaking their words through his mouth. They looked out through his eyes. Myra could see their soul agenda of greed, power, and their lack of emotion.

As she looked through the chanting crowed, she saw the parasites attached to others. She realized that this was happening because the First Family's mission had been detected. Those influences of control were what had kept Tyree enslaved in limit and fear.

Myra shifted her vision and opened her eyes.   She looked out over the crowd gathered in the Council gardens. She knew many of the assembled citizens. She knew their powerlessness, frustration and fear. The Earth had been in the clouds of escalating negativity since the mission of the First Family was discovered. Myra knew that the way back to their original state would require great determination. Would they remember that they were the ones who could choose and change? Would they remember that their future and the life or death of the greater family rested solely in their hands? She wondered, as did Tuma, if their consciousness could be awaked, would be strong enough.

Growing restless, Myra placed her cup on a small garden table and smiled at Tuma as she moved away from him. Maybe the fact that the Council's deliberations were taking so long was hopeful.

When the proposal from the Gegfad's High Priestess Dana had been presented it was vigorously debated. By fostering fear, greedy individuals with parasitic influence had free rein in Earth societies and this plan could end their control. One of the Chief Ministers, Minister Lucas, was especially outraged. Power and greed was central to his life. Undoubtedly he was ruled by parasitics similar to those she had seen in the street. She had often seen their eyes flicker through his.

Myra walked over to a garden bench where she could watch the doors of the Council Chambers. Thinking over the morning, Myra could see Dana. Her speech was designed to spark whatever in Tyreans memories was not dulled by negativity or locked into denial.

All in the room had been transfixed as Dana spoke. She gave no hint that she was aware of the forces against her, indeed, against all of them. However, those on mission knew that her words would trigger anger within those the parasitics controlled. The Gegfad members continually dissipated energy disrupted by the Council's reactions.

Dana had spoken clearly. "We trusted the courageous and creative nature within you, our Galactic family members, to have the strength and determination to accomplish your mission. You were the ones who volunteered and gave your word. From a deep love and vision, you heard the plan and said, "Yes!"

"We did not intend Earth as a place for judgments or duality or war. There was great attention to make a way to remove such influences before life expanded on this new planet. By testing the manifested forms to identify those that would constrict and take away life we would have been free of these influences. Tyree was to be a city of joy and beauty."

Several members of the Earth Council had nodded. Others smoldered with anger. Anxiety and doubt rippled through the Hall. Heavy energy had darkened the room until it was cleared by those on the mission.

Dana had turned, her hand sweeping to include all in the Council as she said, "You are the leaders. How are you leading out of the darkness to implement that Divine plan?"

Then she had paused.

"By divine decree, life on this sphere will always call forth form from word and thought. In this way it will also manifest hidden energies. You can help your people break free of control and transform fear. Their right is to live on this planet in abundance, joy and free will. We offer to stay and help you awaken the consciousness of truth, of purpose and clarity."

Myra sighed and closed her eyes at the memory.

Then, a collective energy shift jarred her back to the present moment.

She looked out over the people. The doors of the Council Chamber were being pushed open as members of the Greater Council moved from the chamber. The robed members filed down the corridor and into the Hall. Those who had wandered into hallways or gardens quickly moved back to their places.

Myra looked toward Tuma and glancing past him she noticed that even those disrupting on the streets had halted. Fists dropped to their sides, quiet whispers replaced shouts as all attention was on the Council members.

The tall young man had moved to stand close to the garden enclosure. The former frenzy replaced with silent confusion.

Myra moved to walk in with Tuma. "Do you think that they will be willing to let us stay and mentor them?" she whispered to Tuma. He tilted his head with raised eyebrows as if to indicate that he thought it was not likely. Stay and assist the transition or go back to their home.

Everyone stood until the Council was seated at the dais facing those in attendance. Any clues as to the outcome of the vote were veiled in the stoic faces of the Council members. Gyra, the leader arose. He was a large man. Myra had come to appreciate his sensitivity to the problems within Tryree. He walked with awareness and was accustomed to political negotiations. Compassionate use of his power and influence had earned him a place of respect among those on mission.

"Speaking for the Council, I want to thank all of you who have been with us during the long hours of debate and discussion. Clearly, this matter is important to you as it is to us.

"I speak to our guests from regions beyond our Earth. There has been much spoken here this day of our beginnings. We appreciate and respect your information. We have contemplated the matter of our future with great attention. Our decision did not come easily."

Gyra paused, cleared his throat and lifted a paper from the table. He looked stooped, Myra thought, weighted with the magnitude of this matter. Before he continued she felt a sudden jolt in her abdomen. She knew the decision.

He took a deep breath and began reading. "It is the decision of the Greater Council of Tyree that those who have shared with us their ways are now to return to their homes. We extend our gratitude for the balancing of our energies and for the exemplary way they have lived among us. But, the course we are on is the one we will pursue. We find no reason to change its direction at this time."

A ripple ran through the Gegfad members, a shudder, and then an acceptance. Myra saw the arrogance on the faces of those Council members who very powerfully manipulated attitudes and perceptions. Half-truths, flattery and outright deceit had swayed the vote. Then, Myra looked at her friend, Dana. Wisdom etched the high priestess's face while sadness filled her eyes.

Myra heard shouts and screams from outside the Council Hall. Through the wide windows she could see that word of the decision had reached the streets. Running, fists thrashing the air, the tall man was again frantically moving through the crowds knocking down any in his way. The smaller groups became a mob with the Rycur authorities trying to maintain control.

Myra turned back to the Hall and caught a glance between Council member Lucas and Dana. Lucas looked smug, lips curled in a smile of triumph. These two leaders represented the extremes of the Earth's energy, parasitic unbridled greed to control and love.

Myra turned and looked out of the windows to the streets, the riots, the shouts and screams. So who had won and what had really been lost?

CHAPTER 3

Stones crashed onto the shields and helmets of the double lines of Rycur forces. Gathered at a rear door, they had been charged to assure the safe exit of members of the Gegfad mission. The streets boiled with clashes between Tyreans angry that the guests were leaving and crowds of those who wanted them gone.

Dana had sent word through the Council Hall and gardens for those of the Gegfad mission to quietly make their way to the conference room at the northwest corner of the Council Hall. Myra silently moved toward the designated room exchanging quick good byes with Tryean friends. The once welcoming city was deteriorating into an uncontrolled mêlée.

As she approached, she could see Tuma watching from the conference door and together they went into the room. In a short time, all Gegfad members were there. The mood in the room was somber, insulated against the disruptions on the street.

"Well, my friends," Dana began. "I am so proud to be a part of this amazing outreach. Your commitment to radiate the true nature of our family despite all cynicism took great courage. You have left a legacy of compassion, grace and peace that will be remembered for generations.

"We have two hours to gather our things. Our ships are standing by and you will have Rycur escorts for your safety. There will be time for discussion later but now we must hurry. Leave quickly and I will see you all onboard."

Myra and Tuma went with a small group out the back of the garden moving into the shadows of the trees at the edge of the crowds. They had almost cleared the second street when they heard shouts and running feet. Myra turned. Through the spaces between the guards she saw the tall blond man running toward them hurling stones and screaming his anger. For just a moment, she looked into his eyes, eyes filled with parasitic hate. Then the Rycur guards blocked his way.

As the ships moved away from the Earth, the intercom signaled for quiet. Those on board each ship stopped their activities to listen. The intercom crackled and the voice of Jerra, the High Priest of their mission, came, "My dear friends," he began. "I greet you from the Galactic Council, the Masters and your brothers and sisters of Light. Our greater family in worlds beyond Earth are aware of your efforts and of the vote by the Tyrean Great Council.

"We are all affected by the Council decisions. Today's vote by the Council is to be discussed at a meeting called by the multi-dimensional Galactic Council. Our commitment to stop Outsider's from sucking our life energy must continue lest they destroy all of us."

Myra couldn't get the blond man's eyes out of her mind. They were staring, empty one minute and red-rimmed, filled with rage the next. She had seen his docile mood, almost confused stance, as he leaned at the fence before the vote. Then, she saw a filling up, a coming alive, but alive to frenzied rage, hostility.

She shuddered and breathed herself back to the present and Jerra's words, "our commitment .... our commitment."

Thinking again of the young blond man she whispered emphatically, "my commitment, this must end!"

After the ships had landed the Gegfad members went to their homes to later attend the Galactic Council meeting. Jerra and Dana sat at the main table. They had been asked to preside.

Soft lights and music filled the open Chamber Hall spilling out into the large spacious gardens. The other members of the Gegfad mission were seated to the left and right of the couple all facing the circle of attendees. The flight home had been uneventful, a time to rest and contemplate the Earth experience. They came to this meeting prepared to hear the next step.

"As you know," Jerra began, "those of Earth heritage, The Ancient Ones and first family, have a unique responsibility for our return to our home star state. The original plan has been compromised and through the many disruptions within the physical body suit, false systems have been imposed. They are operating with crippled energy.

"It is proposed that there be an outreach of those not of the original Earth team. A new mission to enter Earth's evolutionary system, volunteers to be birthed into a physical body as a member of an Earth family. We are hoping that the abilities, and perceptions they have developed in our other world societies will survive the density and be available to them. If it goes as we hope, this will bring new clarity into the Earth families and break through their unconsciousness. As they break free of parasitic constructs, Divine will infuse new possibilities and allow natural expressions of abundance and health."

Whispered exchanges and a ripple of excitement ran through the group.

Jerra continued, "This mission would allow us to remind and awaken the power of light and love in our birth families and awaken skills and abilities more intimately."

Jerra looked around the attentive group. Then he spoke. "We are all aware of the heavy energies that blind and dull Earth. It is critical to assure awareness and connections to Home energy for those on this mission. We have planned a way to counter this denseness for the volunteers. There will be many friends, teachers and masters who will remain in spiritual bodies to guide, direct and give access to the overall plans. This system will bypass the cloudiness of Earth. By tuning into an inner system, each volunteer will have access to clarity for decisions while on planet Earth."

Jerra paused and walked a few steps in quiet thought.

"The ships will be leaving this planet in a fortnight. Those of you who decide to volunteer will want to return home for a short time before beginning this assignment.

"Remember, there is individual choice on Earth. As a member of an Earth family, you will operate to chose and direct your life. Many in spiritual bodies will be available to answer your questions and fulfill your requests, but the universal law functioning on Earth puts the right of creating and changing into the hands of individuals

"We will live within that law. When the volunteers see a need, they can call in unlimited spiritual help to meet the need or correct the problem but there must be a request."

Jerra stopped speaking and turned toward Dana. He smiled at her and she responded with a nod and moved to stand beside him. Myra could sense their love. They were like young lovers with one another even after eons. Myra knew the feelings. Tuma still caused her heart to sing.

Then Jerra went on. "You notice that we are using the word volunteer. This is a freewill undertaking. No one is required to participate."

"As the High Priest, it is my responsibility to hold the vision for this mission and to assure our return home. This mission's purpose is to restore the original plan initiated by those First Family, Ancient Ones. We will expose and remove parasitic energy and assist Earth families to return to the light. I will hold this mission's purpose clearly in mind.

"We strongly urge each of you to go within to contemplate and review. If any have questions, there will be discussions later this evening."

Myra saw Jerra reach for Dana's hand and look into her azure eyes, "Dana and I have chosen to be part of this group." The hall erupted in applause.

Myra looked at Tuma. He was focusing intently on Jerra's words. She recognized his excitement and enthusiasm as it touched her. She laid her hand on his. He gently lifted their joined hands and brushed hers softly with his lips. A smile passed between them and her heart swelled. The choice was made without the need to speak. They would join the volunteers on this unusual opportunity of love.

Eve felt a chill move throughout her body. Goose bumps rose on her skin. Something was not right. She and Adam walked down the path edged with low bushes, sheltered from the hotter rays of the sun by the overhanging branches of the oak. They had walked this path many times before and yet something was off. She looked up at him.

"Do you feel the change in the energy," she asked Adam.

"No," he replied." I am just enjoying the quiet of the garden. What is it that you are sensing?"

"I don't know. Something's different in the garden. It reminds me of the feelings I had yesterday. A few of the forms my teacher had me taste left similar sensations. I know that there is a warning. I remember enough to know that I must be watchful, but of what? Will you trust what I feel?"

"You know that I will. You are the one!" Adam laughed gently and squeezed her hand to reassure her. He acknowledged that she knew more that he did about keeping their garden clear.

Eve walked, eyes open, senses alert.

CHAPTER 4

Myra breathed deeply and let out a laugh that filled the laboratory. Tuma would be on the first wave of the Joehicca mission and was practicing. His team members turned to look at her and she covered her mouth to stifle her giggles.

Watching him maneuver the simulated body suit, one that would be much too small, struck her as outrageously funny. It was all that she could do to keep herself still until the routine was completed and then relief. A major hurdle crossed. Her laughter broke the team's intense concentration and everyone erupted into laughter and cheers.

His planning team members were highly intelligent and yet had not walked this particular path. The Ancients Ones, those who had been the original mission wave, spent time briefing the newest volunteers on what they might encounter. But not all of the Ancient Ones had birthed into corrupted body suits.

The Ancient One, Gogan, had been assigned to Tuma's team. He carried himself with the confidence deepened by his time as a First Family member. He had walked the Earth in true freedom and curiosity. He had watched his mate explore areas of the Mother's surface for a place she loved. He had stood by her side as she identified cycles for support and as she sang energy into food, beauty and abundance. The Ancients knew Earth as the base center of their mission. They had walked in her spaces like none since. Gogan held the remembrance of what was to have been.

Since her life on the planet would interweave with his, Myra was both observer and participant in his plans. She listened to discussions amongst Tuma's team. She observed as calculations were made of the planets affecting Earth was considered in deciding a time of birth that would best support Tuma's mission.

She shook her head at the thought of today's exercise in the simulated body suit, just too much. She laughed again remembering him working to pull all of his energy into the tiny suit and then maneuvering. How to make the hands work, the mouth. What system would coordinate the legs and eyes. After all the numbers and formulas, calculations and theories, it may all come down to one question. Can we maneuver our tiny body suits.

"Sometimes I know that this mission can be accomplished very easily," Tuma said to Myra one day when they were alone. "And yet, it would be foolish to ignore the fact that the leaders in the township where I will birth have great control over the people. Those are the times when I wonder if we can pull it off."

Myra brushed his hair back over his ears. "Well, we know your friends are committed to you and to the success of this mission. The power of our Divine family's commitment to each other is stronger that the energy of chaos and conflict." And as she mouthed the words, the blond hair and hateful eyes of the young man at Tyree came back to her.

Tuma took her into his arms and kissed her lips. He infused her with confidence. Of course, all would go well.

Tuma and Myra walked down the sandy path to their favorite spot, the lake at the foot of the azure crystalline mountains. He held her hand as she made her way around some large boulders to sit on a grassy spot next to the lake. She looked across the water to the rich vegetation and glorious trees. "I love this place," she said to Tuma. "It is so beautiful and peaceful." He settled next to her and they talked of their excitement for what lay ahead.

They sat quietly, Myra leaning against Tuma. "Remember that I will be with your friends as you go. And will watch over you until I come," Myra whispered.

Tuma drew her closer to him. She felt embraced by his love, every part of her being caressed with overwhelming emotions. There was never a question as to her place by his side. This is where she belonged.

"May the time go swiftly until I can hold you again, my love," he whispered.

Encompassing love flowed between them. No part of was left untouched, no part not transformed by this energy that moved, twirled and filled them. Expanded and more one than ever, knowing that they would soon part, they looked at the azure peaks and the greenery of their home.

"Myra, I promise from the depth of my soul to fulfill this mission with speed and integrity. Know that I will be there to help you awaken from Earth's density".

Myra nestled closer to Tuma and tears flowed down her cheeks. They sat quietly, holding and touching.

Myra's birth into a family within the village was planned to occur shortly after Tuma's. She approached her preparation with the same vigor she had seen in Tuma. She had her own team, her own plans. There was a timing issue to be considered, a timing that would bring them together.

One day as Myra was working in her simulated suit, not laughing now that she felt the difficulty. After an especially disconcerting maneuver, she huffed, "It occurs to me that this vehicle pretty well masks my appearance."

Giggling her team members had to agree. The jerky movements were enough to hide Myra's natural grace.

"Then how will Tuma know this is me or for that matter, will I know him?"

The team captain spoke up, " The soul link forged from eons of sharing is a pretty strong bond. We can't complete this mission alone. It is only together, as a team that we can succeed. The goal is every family member awake and return to Home frequency."

Tuma walked into the lab during the discussion. "Remember, it is not intended that we walk this mission alone. The only reason for individual choice is to allow immediate identification of parasitic energy and the right to demand their removal. That will require that we stand in our personal strength. The strength you bring will give me safety and my love will fill you with confidence and grace. When you add the connected spokes of the rest of our family, we succeed. Everyone awake and back to Home frequency."

Her strength and presence would bring safety to him and his love would nurture her. Myra would develop sensitivity to the lighter energies. As Tuma awakened and held healthy frequencies of love, she would clear any hint of negativity. Eventually, Myra and Tuma would join with others on this mission and the expansion will shift Earth inhabitants further away from the grip of darkness. Together they felt confident that they could awaken their community.

One day, the sense of the one Tuma knew as mother came, an inner call. He had sensed her often during her time of carrying. She was a good woman of royal birth. He felt fortunate that he had chosen her. Now, her pains of childbirth pulled to him across the ethers. As he turned to tell Myra, he realized that she already knew.

As Tuma drifted away from her, Myra extended into the slower frequencies of Earth to be by the young mother's side. With encouraging words she told Tuma's mother of the love her new son would bring. She told of his gifts and mission. Although her ears, dulled from Earth density, could not translate the words, the young mother sensed Myra's presence as a wave of calm and she relaxed.

Traveling into a dark, dense space, Tuma sped away from the light. He felt heaviness and fear. Then Tuma saw his beloved Myra touching the hand of the one he would call mother. In the next moment he was pulled toward his physical vehicle and sucked into its very small space. Strange energy fields seemed to supersede his own and what was once familiar became confused. He was swimming, grasping. Something felt wrong, but what was it? There were energies clouding his mind.

The pains for him and his mother were intense. He had moved in and out of the body on many occasions during her time of carrying. Those times he had felt cradled, comforted by the constant beat of his mother-to-be's heart. But, birth was a shock to his entire being. He felt pain, fear and confusion.

Myra sensed Tuma's panic, his bewilderment. She instantly cleared the waves. She was not unaffected as her own fears crept in. Were they really doing the wise thing? Would they be able to stay clear? As quickly as the doubts arose, she felt them soften and lift. She turned. Dana stood by her side.

"Those who have committed to guide Tuma are friends of integrity. They will watch over him. We are stepping into the unknown, but there is much hope for the outcome," Dana comforted.

Myra turned back to the birth scene. Tuma had taken his first breath as a member of an Earth family. His mother held him. She smiled and then, weary with the hours of labor, the new mother closed her eyes and slept.

In the days after Tuma's birth, Myra watched, missing him terribly. Lovingly, her heart reached out to him for the moment they would be together in their earthly adventure.

Tuma's Earth family had various reactions to his presence. His mother's mood would change with simply a look and a smile from her son. Others felt calmed as they held and rocked him. But, his father, Driva, was not happy with this new male infant. Driva, the grandson of the one whom Myra had known as Lucas, was every bit a product of his grandfather's power-hungry genetics. But, unlike his grandfather who used words to deceive, Driva simply took. His parasitic nature brought enslavement and pain to all around him. Driva felt exhilarated by power and control. It was his reason for living. The weakness of others, their groveling and fear, enabled Driva to demand, to take and to give nothing in return.

Tuma, who was now called Behra, was Driva's first-born son. He would be the one to carry on the family line with its titles and lands. Driva would allow no smiles. He called such exhibitions weakness. Any plea to acknowledge the small one's presence was met with cold rebuke or physical abuse. Driva treated his wife harshly and ignored his son.

He decided that as soon as Behra was weaned he, Driva, would take over the child's training.

Myra watched as Tuma's body suit began to store the traumatic energy around him. His energy fields began to register the lack he felt within. His spiritual friends called to him, reminded him and encouraged him to stay strong. He often heard their calls, moving his body with the excitement and relief he felt. His movements appeared like clever actions of a happy baby. Behra's mother softly caressed his cheeks, whispered her love and encouraged his play.

For a time, Behra remembered the words, "Earth is a free-will planet and those not in physical bodies have no right to act if not invited." Communicating with his friends through thoughts sent over the ethers, Behra asked for their help. He tried to remember what to ask and how to listen, But his memory soon clouded, a result of the negative energy around Earth, within his home and the disruptions in his circuitry systems.

CHAPTER 5

Driva stormed into the nursery. His velvet robes spread out behind him like the wings of an enormous bird. The click of his heavy boots shook the room.

Three-year-old Behra's eyes opened wide in fright. He cowered behind his mother's skirt. Swooped up in large rough, hands, Behra hung in mid air not daring to breath. Just as quickly he was dropped into the arms of his father's manservant.

"Gather his clothes, his bedding, " boomed his father. "He will be staying with the men from now on."

Behra watched in terror and confusion as his mother pleaded and wept. The servants scurried to gather his things tying them into bundles as Driva bellowed and commanded.

The loss of his mother created a deep wound within young Behra. Even with her, it had taken all of his strength to find ways to survive; now the constant presence of his cruel father caused immense fear and pain. It was easier to deny his Light, to do as his father wished and to forget any dream of ending the hopelessness that was everywhere around him. He was so small and his father was so immense.

It was then that Myra was born into her family. Unlike the wealth and royalty of Behra's Earth family, Myra was born into very impoverished conditions. Her family was one of the least within the village.

As Myra moved away from the light and entered the birth process she felt great restrictions. Her energy seemed to slow and the world she entered was cold and heavy.

Tears rolled down Myra's tiny checks. Her parents wondered at their beautiful sleeping daughter. Were these tears of enchantment? Certainly not sadness in one so young. Perhaps she had a slight illness. They rocked her small bed and hushed any fears.

Remembering Tuma's distress, Myra called out. "Dana, I need some help. The circuitry within this body is wrong!"

"I'll see what I can find out," Dana reassured her. "It may take a little time, but I will be back."

Myra's tears slowed. She drifted into an uneasy sleep and from that inner place she reached to Behra. She knew that she could reach into his heart, jog a memory, cause a response that had a softening effect on him. It gave her a sense of comfort. She would hold this connection while she waited to hear from Dana.

Dana followed the lines of energy moving from the top of Myra's small body. She watched lights move through tiny threads that wove, crossed and connected. They knew that there had been some re-engineering. The Council's plans had taken these disruptions into consideration, but as she compared what she saw in Myra's tiny body to the Divine pattern, Dana was dumbfounded.

The Galactic Council had hoped that birthing into physical body, would change the energy by over riding the crippled circuitry. But no one had considered that the body systems were so disrupted. What would this mean for the Joehicca mission?

Dana reported back to Myra.

"My friend, what I have found is very shocking. Now, remember this is my first scan and I am going back to the Council to go over these figures and configurations with the experts there. We may have to do some trouble shooting as the mission progresses, but we can do that if you keep calling to us for help."

Myra's tears returned with shaking sobs. Her mother lifted her from the cradle to calm and nurse her precious daughter. Myra would not be comforted and cried without relief. Finally, tired and weak, she could no longer stay awake. Her cries slowly subsided with the rocking of her mother's body. Assured that Myra would be okay until it was decided what needed to be done; Dana kissed the top of the small baby head and moved away.

Dana had not wanted to alarm Myra. There was nothing that her friend could do at this point. Dana needed more information. She had found that wiring for spiritual communications was overlaid with some disruptive device; the emotional flow was now routed through the mental center. The power center was disconnected totally and would never function in its present state. The evolutionary circuitry was blocked. The steps that had so carefully been coded into the DNA had been disconnected from the basic centers. The change would make it virtually impossible to move from survival on this new planet into the abilities needed to connect to the soul vision, one's place in greater society and then to the higher evolutionary path.

She was silent, contemplating the information. As Dana realized the gravity of the situation, tears welled up in her eyes and her heart felt constricted and painful.

"Do you know what this means?" Dana spoke to herself, panicked at what she had seen. "Myra is stuck in a crippled body with no way to accomplish her mission. If Jerra has a body similar in any way, he can never accomplish his. What about Tuma and the others? How widespread is this crippling?"

Dana knew that answers to these questions were critical. She also realized that Myra's systems would become mired if she were to panic. Dana shifted her focus to Behra and Jerra. To her dismay, she found their circuitry as badly confused as Myra's. Behra was clouded because of the damage. In addition, he now struggled with the effect of the density of his home. Myra had been clear enough to ask for help.

Returning to her home, Dana asked to speak to the Galactic Council. She stood before this august group and began a report of Myra's request and of her findings. Her words carried a sense of urgency. The members listened and asked questions that revealed concern. But, there was not the shock that Dana had anticipated. She wondered if they realized the gravity of the problems.

Sela, the President of the Council, leaned forward across the Council table. Her words were a response to Dana's unasked question.

"Yes, dear one, as you know we were aware of the problems in the circuitry. We had hoped that the Light bodies would override the crippling. Since that is not happening, other plans are ready.

"A two pronged healing mission is to be undertaken. It will involve a portion of the volunteers. They will be birthed as planned, but with additional assignments. This segment will active the Sihedaa work."

Dana listened intently.

Jeon, another Galactic Council member, stood, walked around the table and continued.

"At a given time, the Sihedda members will be encouraged to awaken to their true identity. The deep sense of love and unity, the natural state of our Galactic family they carry, will be the awareness to a spark that ignites a quest.

"Pain may be the motivation. Seeing themselves and others trapped in a way they do not understand, they will search for answers. That quest will be to find the cause of humanity's unrelenting limits and pain, not to just understand it. With each request, those of us in spirit support can help inform, release and transform the density. Eventually, ownership by the parasitic societies will be remembered, contracts eliminated and the survival patterns transformed. The limits created from lifetimes among the Earth families will be lifted.

"The goal of the Sihedda group is not to convince others, but to remember their Divinity, to hold fast to their inner knowing and to ask to be returned to Divine vibrations. We will work together to remind them of all has been hidden. Anything that results in chaos and distorted energy will be revealed. Then, we can work together to create ways to transform or eliminate disruptive forces. Once that is done, this group will lead the way as the other mission volunteers awaken.

"This group will be taught what has been hidden, remember information, speak words to reawaken their Divine selves and anchor new energy vortexes to the planet. Their awareness will draw them together in a conscious group around the planet. At their request, the appropriate re-wiring of energy circuitry will be done. They will integrate with their soul identity, restructure their circuitry and be empowered to stand in their full glory. Waking to their wholeness, they can act as surrogates for the other volunteers.

"With their right to make choices in this planet, these volunteer who have been in the life stream of Earth bodies can then say, 'This is our home by adoption, Evil and fear are no longer allowed. There can no longer be abuse, neglect or mistreatment. Earth is a sphere for all to experience peace, abundance and joy, Now! All lack, hate, war and deception is revealed for what it is, falseness and entrapment. We command that it be banished from this galaxy! We demand a return to Earth's original plan and glory.' "

As Dana heard the proposal, she grasped at the magnitude of the endeavor.

"And are the volunteers for this portion of the task known?" she asked.

"Yes and the number of volunteers are significant. Those who first awaken, transform and anchor the vortexes will be few, but those who follow and step into wholeness will be many. Then, a power shift will occur in consciousness for all of Earth's inhabitants. It will be as if they suddenly wake up and recognize their true nature. They will effortlessly create peace, beauty, trust and abundance. Earth will lighten and exist as the sphere she was intended to be. It is a monumental undertaking. We need not tell you how critical it is for the Earth and for the galaxy."

Jeon paused and looked back at the other Council members.

Now, Sela leaned forward.

"Dana, we are asking you to lead the Sihedaa mission."

Dana reeled. She searched the faces of those around her. What were they asking?

Sela stood and walked toward Dana. She moved effortlessly. Taking Dana's hands into her own, she looked deeply into Dana's eyes.

"We need you there."

Dana's mind raced. How much time did she have to consider? Could she do this? Then she stopped. She was thinking by Earth's rules. Here, her assignment was given and she would accept.

How she longed for Jerra. She called to him through the ethers and on the Earth; a small boy suddenly looked up from his studies. What a strange feeling, he thought.

And then, he went back to his assigned task puzzled at the buzzing he felt through his body. "I'm hungry," he concluded, trying to explain what he felt.

Eve kicked the loose sand with her feet as she walked with Adam. The nagging feeling was still with her and marred the peace she usually felt in their garden. She slowed her pace, thinking about what her Ancient teacher had introduced.

Her teacher had reminded Eve that in this world there were societies of Outsiders who constricted the vibrancy of life. As she thought, Adam moved a little ahead of her. He was rounding the bend when Eve looked up. She hurried to catch up to him.

And then she felt it, a whish, an uncomfortable blow to her belly, her wisdom center. Eve held the energy spot as she stopped to catch her breath. She felt light headed, a bit dizzy.

As she stood, her eyes locked on the eyes of a stranger. He was standing ahead on the path.

Adam looked at her, not understanding. He reached out for her hand and together they walked forward to the place where the stranger stood, smiling.

Eve felt the cold move throughout her body. Goose bumps rose on her skin and her hair stood on end.

Her mind swirled. She was so new at this. This stranger looked okay. Adam was not alarmed. What should she do?

And before she could decide, the stranger spoke to Adam. "Have you ventured beyond the limits I imposed?" he said.

And the world went black as Eve collapsed onto the ground.

CHAPTER 6

With each lifetime on the Earth, the Gegfad members birthed into bodies and found themselves in reoccurring situations. Sexual abuse by a parent in one life took the form of abuse by a spouse in another. Anger and rage at a mother's unfulfilled promise of protection became an unreasonable distrust of women in the next. Death from rocks hurled by an angry mob became dull back pains in another lifetime.

And so the Gegfad volunteers who came to free the planet experienced the power of parasitic enslavement and debilitating experiences from the unending fear. In each lifetime, it appeared unbidden and sabotaged their lives. Earth's density dimmed their consciousness. Their Divine gifts seemed like dream possibilities and cynicism replaced hope.

With their fractured memory of home, Earth life was empty. The mission members buried parts of themselves to survive. And began to live with the questions, "Who am I?" "Why am I here?" "Can't others see the craziness of this place?" "What is my mission?" "Will I recognize the call?" "When can I go Home?"

Their Spiritual friends continued to speak to them, but the curtain of darkness became denser and the frequency that carried the spiritual counsel was distorted. The words were lost.

They felt isolated, abandoned and pain at the insanity on the planet. At various times, they tried to step out of the density and the pain, but the distorted wiring, false body patterns kept them stuck.

Tuma/Rory

Rory felt shaken. He was troubled by the events of the afternoon. His years as a counselor had been moderately satisfying, not fulfilling in the way he had hoped. Too many clients slipped deeper into despair, the casualties of society. It seemed to be getting worse. How could he help them and stop the escalation?

This feeling was not new. What was disconcerting were the inner pictures that had begun to come to him lately, dreams he had assured himself. But, this afternoon the new woman at the Center had unnerved him. Her eyes and the dreams were somehow connected. Now he was concerned. The images were no longer only night visions.

Myra/Gerri

Gerri wept, holding her dog close. What was the matter with people? Her parents said she was too sensitive. "No need to be all upset at others' pain. Life is not always easy or just. There are more important things to worry about, like school assignments and plans for the future, " they said.

But, Gerri's heart cried out. Why the pain? She saw hurt everywhere and asked, "Why?"

People were so isolated and hostile. Their pessimism made the world ugly.

"Why?" echoed throughout her being.

Jerra/Bob

Bob slipped his backpack to the ground and stretched. He threw his arms out and sucked in the mountain air, the scent of trees, water and wild flowers.

This made life worthwhile! He lived for the weekends to get away from the rush of the city with it's isolated living. He loved the peace and beauty of his mountains.

How long had it been since his last visit – two months?

No, three! Much too long.

Dana/Pam

Pam leaned on the pole for support. Her head throbbed.

"To hell with life!" she thought. "I'm through! From now on I fight like everyone else. Whatever I need to do to survive, I'll do. There's no one but me to take care of me!"

She thought her father would never stop! And where was her Mom? Just where she had always been working in the kitchen as if nothing was wrong! Her anger at the man she had known as father was surpassed by the rage she felt at her mother.

She'd never go back, no matter what she had to do!

CHAPTER 7

As he walked, Rory was lost in thought. He turned the corner and headed toward his apartment complex.

Slipping the key into the apartment lock, he paused.

"Get a grip on yourself. You encounter situations like this every working day. Why has this one thrown you a curve?"

He thought for a moment and then breathed a sigh of relief. Of course. It was Friday. The week had been hectic, new clients, court cases. He just needed a break to recoup.

Smiling, he turned the key. The apartment door opened to his cozy home. Rory bent, picked up the evening paper from the mat, stepped inside and closed the door.

He dropped the paper and keys on the hall table as if shedding the outside world.

Heading into his bedroom, Rory kicked off his shoes and flopped onto the bed. He had no time constraints for the entire weekend. His tired muscles relaxed and his mind drifted.

Soon he was breathing deeply and slowly.

From far away, Rory hear a sound, a phone ringing. Not far away, his phone. It jarred him back to the bedroom and shaking off sleep he reached to answer.

"Dr. James?" came the voice over the line.

"Yes." Rory cleared his throat, trying to sound alert and professional.

"It's the woman we admitted this afternoon. She's insisting she must leave. We have orders to notify you of any changes."

"I'll be right down. Give me five minutes," he said.

He placed the phone back in its cradle as he scooted his feet around in search of his shoes.

Dr. Rory James grabbed his car keys and rushed out of the door.

Rory's work extended beyond his regular office hours. The Center was an additional project to assist individuals in trouble, a place for the emotionally wounded. It provided time, space and support as they turned their lives around. It had been a brainchild of his and many had been helped during the last three years.

Five minutes later, he pulled into his parking space at the Center. He walked briskly down the corridors to room 20A. This young woman had been brought in by a friend on the police force. She had been living on the streets, had broken no laws, but indicated that she wanted help. Wanting help was enough to get space at the Center.

So why was the woman in 20A different?

He knocked gently on the door before he turned the knob and entered the room.

The young woman he knew only as Pam was huddled at the head of her bed. Her arms wrapped around her knees, softly crying and rocking. Her pain filled the small room.

Rory's heart went out to her.

"Pam," he spoke her name softly.

She seemed not to hear him.

He had found it very beneficial, at times, to simply be with his clients, let their actions guide. He pulled up a chair and began to slowly rock. Then, softly his sounds matched her sounds and they blended. Her eyes stared ahead as if seeing into windows he could not reach. He also gazed ahead and rocked.

Time passed. It seemed as though, together, they gave voice to the pain of millions: the sadness, the helplessness, and the abuse of so many. Soon, his cries were his own, for friends lost, for patients untouched, for society's limits.

Slowly, her rocking and her crying stopped.

Pam's eyes focused on Rory as if seeing him for the first time. He looked back into eyes that had haunted him from his earlier encounter. Azure eyes, so deep and wise, with such sadness. A sense of loss lay within the blue and he felt pain for all those he had not been able to reach. A wail rose up from deep within his heart and gave way in a sob he could not suppress.

At his cry, she turned her eyes to the window and laid her head upon her knees and wept.

Slowly, he composed himself, reached out and placed his hand gently on her head.

"You cannot go. This is your place to be for now," Rory assured.

His heart swelled with some unknown love and familiarity. Words tumbled from his mouth, "We need you here."

"I know," she whispered and lay down on the bed and slept.

Far away, in a more serene setting, Bob gathered firewood as he walked; it was a good way to keep dead branches cleaned up. He leaned the smaller branches over a nest of kindling; he felt such satisfaction when the campfire lit with just one match, a carryover from his scouting days, no doubt.

The fire caught and lapped up the teepee of twigs. Bob added larger sticks. He watched the flames twist and turn, change shape, reach out for more fuel, and finally settle into a steady source of heat. The gyrating fire mesmerized him. It was part of the intrigue and healing of these weekends.

Then, the beautiful azure eyes came back to haunt him. They danced as the smoke curled. They laughed as the embers burned. Then, they became heavy and sad and slowly disappeared into the dark of night.

Bob was shaken. It was as if her cry sounded from across the world to him and he was unable to run to her side. Although not a religious man, he was a very spiritual being. He called out to all he knew that was good; the trees, the birds, the stream and the moon hanging low in the sky, "Take care of my love wherever she is tonight. Keep her safe. Whisper to her soul of my love."

He stared into the fire as tears fell from his eyes. Loneliness, from some deep inner place, spread throughout his chest. Bob sat next to the fire and sobbed. What did it mean?

For eons as High Priest, I have held the vision for the Earth as well as for the various missions from the Galactic Family. My heart calls out into the silence of this great planet. I call for all to search their heart. Are you a part of this mission?"

Now, I need others to hold these visions with me. I long for them to come forward and stand together in strength and clarity. Our planet and its inhabitants are crying for healthy caregivers. She needs those who hear her cries to powerfully say, "No" to invasion, to deceit and to tyrannical power.

Not only is the Earth being damaged but our societies are in great trouble. From individuals to schools systems, from businesses to governments, the effects of destructive attitudes and behaviors are everywhere.

The present moment is a time of great power. From this point in time and space, we can bring all dimensions to wholeness, transformed powerfully. We have the right to demand a return to free agency, uniqueness, love and peace.

I declare our Divine sovereignty!

Please hear me!

CHAPTER 8

Pam's dreams had taken her back to where it had begun. Pain pounded in her head with the memories of father's beatings, the rape, the powerlessness. For so long she had blocked those days to survive. Pam closed her eyes and the foggy memories gave way. And then came last night. The doctor had come, sat by her bed, cried and stayed. Did someone finally understand? The thought of safely was almost more than she could bear. He had come, he had cried, and he had stayed. Tears welled up and spilled down her face with the enormity of the experience. Pam closed her eyes and drifted.

It was dusk when she finally awoke. For a few moments she lay very still, orientating herself to the room. A soft knock. She looked up as a woman in her mid-fifties looked in through the partially opened door.

"Hello, you have been sleeping for quite a while. How are you feeling?"

Pam cleared her throat.

"A little hungry, actually."

"Well, that can be remedied. There was homemade vegetable soup for dinner and the cook makes wonderful rolls. Would you like milk or coffee?"

Pam closed her eyes. How long had it been since she had tasted fresh soup with homemade rolls?

"Milk would be wonderful, thank you."

The door closed. Pam slowly sat up and looked around the room. Her bundle was where she had left it. Her coat hung in clear view in the small closet.

She swung her feet off the bed and eased up to make her way into the bathroom. At the sight of the mirror, she quickly turned away. Pam avoided mirrors. They reflected what she did not want to acknowledge.

She felt dizzy. She sat to relieve her body and held her head until the swirling stopped. Then she stood to wash her face and run her fingers through her short brown hair. She almost laughed. The vision of long auburn curls flashed through her mind. She paused for a moment before opening the door to move back to her bed.

There was a knock on the door as the same woman opened it carefully. Balancing a tray of food that made Pam's mouth water, she said, "Here you go.

"By the way, my name is Mary Ann." Pam smiled at the slight Southern lilt and she shifted so the tray fit over her lap. "If you need anything, just push the button on your bed. Dr. James will be in after you've eaten." Then straightening up, Mary Ann asked, " Is there anything else I can get you?"

Pam shook her head, "No, and thank you."

Mary Ann closed the door softly. Pam's hands shook as she broke a piece from the roll, dipped it in the hot soup. Putting it in her mouth, Pam savored every part of the small bit of bread.

"Oh, please let this be the time," she whispered and took her time with the food. A symbol of a new start she hoped.

Finishing, Pam lay back on the pillow. She stared past the tray, past the wall, into scenes beyond this room. The words came back. Words she had heard often during the very hardest times.

"We need you there."

When the anguish and hurt had been more than she thought she could bear, she had sobbed and asked why." Why was she in this family, in this life?"

And there was a quiet voice, "We need you there."

She had stayed, when she would rather have given up.

And what had the doctor said, or was that just another dream?

Pam cleared her mind and brought back the memory. No. It wasn't a dream.

He had reached out to touch her hair and then he had said, "This is your place. We need you here."

Tears welled up in her eyes. What did it all mean? Could her life really fit back together? Would she be able to do it all?

She slid down carefully under the bed tray, lay facing the wall, and closed her eyes again.

Pam was slightly aware that the dinner tray was being removed, but she was in some faraway place, walking in woods. Not alone, but who was with her? She felt safe, happy and she didn't want to come back.

Pam went further into the dream.

CHAPTER 9

From the beginning Gerri had felt like a foreigner. Not much in this world made sense. She knew that her parents were concerned. She spent too much time alone. She avoided people; hard to make friends that way.

She wouldn't go to church either. She told her parents that she could not believe in a God like their minister described. A benevolent being would not judge and punish. When she was about five, she had shared some of her experiences with them, the colors around everything, friends that no one else could see, music that filled the air. They had been shocked and told her never to speak of such things. And so she had held all that was so real and valuable to her inside. Why would anyone prefer this life of fear and blame to the one that was so real to her – one of joy, beauty and acceptance.

In her world, differences were acknowledged and celebrated. No one would hurt another because of one's thoughts. Actions added to or diminished every other being. Encouragement included everyone. She would not live the crazy life she saw around her. If it meant being alone in this strange, hostile place, so be it. She had maintained her high school grades and college seemed to pose no problem and yet at times Gerri felt depressed.

Gerri sat on the grass of the University quad. Her fellow students moved constantly around campus. Some were in groups, others alone.

Couples held hands as they walked or chatted under trees or by their cars. Couples sharing and laughing touched some place inside. Today she felt empty. Would there ever be someone with whom she could feel safe? Would there be someone who didn't demand that she change, who could hear of her dreams and ideas without judgment or derision? If not, she would be alone and her wish to have a partner would remain safely tucked away.

No one would guess at the pain she sensed radiating from campus. She felt it, had always felt it. It was a burden and blessings. It kept her on guard, protective and yet separate. Feeling like such an alien made for a lonely life.

She had avoided people for so long that she wondered if she would ever be able to make friends. Sometimes she missed that part of life and at other times she was glad she didn't have to worry about all the pitfalls. But today, a great sadness engulfed Gerri. She gathered her books and headed for the parking lot.

A small group of young men were walking on the sidewalk ahead of her, laughing and jostling each other. She tucked her head down and quickened her pace. As she approached, they whistled and called out to her. She made her way around them. She felt like her clothes were being pulled away, her body exposed. She pulled herself so deep inside that her heart and lungs constricted. These intense feelings were the burden of her sensitivity. The jeering eyes of one young man caught hers as she rushed by. The eyes only confirmed her judgments.

Fuming, Gerri flung her books onto the back seat of her car. What a crude world. She climbed behind the wheel and slammed the car door. She laid her head against the steering wheel and gripped it until her fingers turned white.

"I'll never, never, never be a part of this sick society!" she spoke through clenched teeth. She was surprised at her rage and alarmed at the undercurrents of fear that she felt.

Starting the car, Gerri drove quickly and soon pulled into the driveway of her home. She opened the car door and pushed up the seat to retrieve her books. A sense of invasion and derision stayed with her. The tall blond was the leader. She could tell by the look in his eyes. His glance wasn't the innocent playfulness of the others. His menacing eyes stirred something in her. Gerri wanted nothing to do with him.

She turned and ran up the stairs to the front door. She stopped to check the mailbox on the porch before opening it and going inside. Gerri hadn't noticed the small foreign car following her from school. Its driver traveled at a safe distance. He parked and watched as she pulled into the driveway and opened the door. The tall, blond man smiled to himself as he made a note of her address and drove away.

Gerri had no idea that eyes were watching her during the day: playing with her dog; walking to the neighborhood store; lounging in the back yard when no one else was at home; studying at the school library until it closed at night. He watched and he waited. He had no idea why he was so obsessed with this strange woman. He had been with others. He found great pleasure in the conquest and in the subservience he found in them. He moved easily from one to another, taking pride in the trail of hurt and anguish he left behind. Life was a game – a game of the powerful and the powerless. He was powerful and would take all that he could. When the time was right, he would make his move and she too would be his. He smirked at the thought.

Weeks later, Gerri was studying late. The library was more crowded than usual. "Must be last minute cramming for mid-terms," she thought. She looked up at the clock. Only fifteen minutes before the 10 p. m. closing. There was one more book she wanted to check for information; there was no time to read through it here.

"I'd better find the book on the shelves and check it out," Gerri reasoned.

She rose quickly and moved to the book aisles. Scanning the top shelves for the title she wanted, Gerri missed the movement of someone behind her.

"Hi, gorgeous!"

Gerri whirled, narrowly missing his chest with her pen. She looked up into the eyes of blond from the sidewalk incident weeks before. Her jaw set, and she turned back to the shelves of books.

"Thought you might like to be walked to your car. It gets rather dark this time of night."

His crooked smile had deceived many, but Gerri was not taken in. Her whole body sensed danger. Her eyes shot him her answer and she turned to walk away. He put out his arm to stop her, but it was too late. He stood feeling angry and embarrassed as he watched her gather her books and leave the library.

This was not what he had expected, not what he would accept. Something deep within took over. He moved swiftly and quietly out the door. He knew her driving path. He knew the shortcut she always took through the small alley.

Driven by some compulsive determination, he climbed into his small car and sped ahead, his blood pounding. This woman was his and he would have her.

As Gerri slowed her car to turn into the alley, the driver's side door was yanked open and a hand reached for the keys to her car.

Later, looking back she thought, "I could have screamed; should have fought". But it all happened so quickly, so unexpectedly.

She was being pulled from the car, held from behind. A dirty cloth was stuffed into her mouth. The rough gravel of the road tore at her skin as she was forced to the ground and her blouse ripped open. Gerri struggled against the strong hands that fondled her breast and forced her jeans down.

The pain of the rape, the threat, the fear and the shame pierced a curtain over a long ago memory. Her emotions rose and ripped open a chamber she had sealed off lifetimes ago. Light filled the chamber and pain echoed throughout her body. Faces flashed on the ceiling of her mind and when the cries stopped, she felt as silent and cold as a faraway star. Gerri went inside an inner cave, burying her self where no one could reach her.

Finished, Dean, the blond young man, collapsed on her. Totally spent, he hurriedly stood up, zipped his jeans and buckled his belt.

Although her face was turned away, he saw that her eyes were closed. In the light of the moon, he could see the blood where her cheek had hit a rock. For a moment he was confused, as if coming out of a bad dream, but he pushed that aside.

"You tell anyone and I'll kill you," he snarled, as he moved to his car, hidden in the shadows.

"She asked for it. The bitch! Just like all women. They have to be taught their place."

He turned the keys to his sports car and sped toward his home.

In his cozy apartment, Rory had just finished reviewing some ideas he had to discuss with the Board of Trustees of the Center. It was 10:25, very little evening left. He got up from his desk to gather all the papers into his briefcase for tomorrow's meeting.

Suddenly, his stomach felt like he had been kicked. He doubled over and his vision blurred. Bile rose in his throat and he swallowed hard. A moan came from a place beyond this physical body. And pictures came. Visions? Dreams? He could not say. His head swirled and the bile come again. A woman. Some long-ago time. Just like before but this time he was holding her. Rocking her limp, unresponsive body. Cries broke loose from the depth of his soul. It radiated throughout his body. And then all he saw was blackness.

Staggering to his bedroom, he sat down on the bed. Holding his head, closing his eyes he tried to comprehend what was happening. He had seen her face before. It was always the same face. He had never before felt the pain, held her body close to his, or known the overwhelming sense of loss. This time he was left with a gapping wound, a great aching emptiness.

CHAPTER 10

Rory had not slept much. For hours he had lain awake with the vision, shaken and helpless. He realized that this pain had been with him for a long time. Buried.

After tossing, unable to push away his sense of loss, Rory got up. As he straightened the scattered papers and placed them in his briefcase he knew that this pain had driven him into counseling.

Toward morning he dozed off. The phone interrupted his troubled dreams.

He rolled over. He read his digital clock as he reached out for the phone. 7 a.m.

"Hello," he cleared his throat and waited.

"Hello, Rory?" His police friend's voice sounded tired. "Sorry to call you at home, but there was a rape last night and I wondered if you might see the young woman. She's twenty-three, extremely traumatized and not speaking. Her parents are very concerned and we need some information."

"Why, sure, Tom. It happened last night you said?"

"Yeah, a college student on her way home from a late night at the campus library. Don't usually get involved this way, but I thought of you right away," Tom responded.

"It's that soft heart that beats beneath the blues, my friend," Rory joked. Then he became the professional, "Have her parents call my office. I'll tell Nora to schedule me some time." Rory really liked Tom. He had sent others to the Center.

"You may have to make a hospital call. She's still there," Tom said.

"I'll do it."

"Thanks, Rory. Sometimes we win. I hope that we can turn this one around for this kid." And the softhearted police officer with the strength to walk in tough places, hung up.

Nora had made arrangements for Rory to visit with the young woman's parents before he went to meet her. They were distraught, blamed themselves, and didn't know what to do. They were appreciative of his expertise, and welcomed his offer to visit with their daughter.

As he entered her hospital room, the young woman's face was turned toward the wall. Rory sat by her bed. She was quiet, her eyes closed and her body lifeless.

Rory gently spoke.

"Gerri. I'm Dr. James."

There was no response.

"I am a friend of Sergeant Palmer, the officer who helped you last night. I have talked with your parents and would like to help you in any way I can. I do not know your pain. How can I? But I am so sorry for what happened to you. I am here for whatever you want or need from me."

Gerri heard his words. Her mind tightened. I will not relive last night, she thought. I will not tell anyone about those eyes and the ripping pain. I will never trust this world.

His words went unanswered. Rory's heart went out to her. There was something very familiar to him. He sat quietly in his own world, as she was quiet in hers. He felt the remnants of last night's pain in his gut. He breathed into the tight muscle and sat for over an hour. Finally, he rose. He touched Gerri's small hand. "I will be back. You are not alone, I promise. I will help you walk through this experience."

Gerri held back tears as he walked out of the room. An old memory or was it a wish?

Myra, I promise from the depth of my soul to fulfill this mission with speed and integrity. Know that I will be there to help you awaken from Earth's density.

CHAPTER

Could she do this?

Pam showered and changed into clean clothes. She was beginning to feel safe in this place they called the Center. Was that smart?

A soft knock at the door and Dr. James come in.

"Hi," he said. "How about going to my office for our talk? Is that okay with you?"

She smiled and nodded. They walked down the hall together and she thanked him for being there.

"It has been so long since I have let anyone see me cry," she began.

"I appreciate your willingness to let me be there and to risk sharing your emotions," Rory responded.

He opened his office door and stood aside as she went in.

"This chair is the best in the room," he laughed and signaled for her. She sat down and he sat on the small sofa close by.

He asked about her needs. Did she want to contact any family members? What professional help had she received? Did she know what she wanted next?

She looked thoughtfully into his eyes.

Rory felt a strange mixture of sorrow and gladness. It was like meeting a long ago friend; seeing that the years had not been kind. He knew she had experienced pain. With difficulty, his professional mind moved that personal feeling aside. He wanted distance and clarity for this woman.

For Pam, it was as if she were weighing him. Making a decision, she took a deep breath, closed her eyes and then began.

"Dr. James, my life has been anything but easy. Some would say it has been unjustly cruel. There was a time when I cursed and raged at God for giving me breathe. But, there has been much that I have learned. I have seen visions that encouraged me to not die. I understood reasons for my situations, at least partially,

"I have shared with no one even a portion of what I have experienced. And yet, something tells me that you will listen, you are to know, and in the telling, I will continue my healing. My question to you is, 'Are you willing to listen?'"

Rory heard her question and with no hesitation answered. "Yes, I am willing."

Pam leaned back, searching her thoughts. Where to start? She had never tried to put her experiences into words or even into a sequence. What would come first?

With her eyes closed, Pam began.

"Ten years ago I was a senior in high school. I loved school. I had a lot of friends. It was my place of safety from my life at home. No one knew that my stepfather was not the gentle man that he presented to the community.

"Three months of school remained before I was to graduate. I planned to work at my part-time job during the summer. I had been accepted at a university and would start the following fall.

"The school was perfect. It was out-of-state, away from my home."

Pam shifted in her chair.

"It was after school on a Friday evening; I had a lot of homework and was scheduled to work full shifts over the weekend. Mom, Dad and I had eaten dinner. I cleared the table and helped Mom with the dishes. She was very quiet. Her silence was always a sign that Dad was in one of his moods. Mom had been with him since I was two, and had learned to stay out of his way then he was *on edge* as she called it."

Pam's voice drifted with the memory. Then catching herself, she came back to her story.

"The man I called Dad was actually my stepfather. My real father had left before I was born. My stepfather owned the local lumberyard. Everyone saw him as a pillar in the community: everyone's friend, someone to look up to. But that was not what we saw at home. He had a cruel side. At home he would explode at the slightest upset. It might be something a customer did; orders that were difficult to fill; overtime to meet deadlines. Anything we did or said could set him off.

"He would beat my mother where no one could see the bruises. She was afraid of him, made excuses, blamed herself and pretended that everything was great.

"He started hitting me when I was little. He told my mother that God made the *man* responsible for his family and that he would sure as hell make me know right from wrong.

"And so, regularly, for twelve years, I watched as he beat my Mom. I learned to cower and hide from him. For sure I had my share of *trainings*.

"When I turned twelve, he became more verbally and physically abusive to me. As I matured, he made cruel remarks about my body, and degraded my school achievements. The beatings increased.

"My senior year was especially hard. I got a part-time job. That helped. It kept me away from home. Keeping on top of my studies as well as my work schedule when home was so ugly, took all the energy and focus I had.

"That Friday," Pam stopped, searched her thoughts and then, breathing deeply, went on.

"That Friday, he ranted a bit through the house. I thought I could stay out of his way because I had so much homework. After dinner and the dishes, I had folded the dishtowel and gone to my room to study when I heard him stomping down the hall. I walked over and closed my door.

"The next thing I knew, he had crashed through my door and stormed in. He was pulling me out from my desk by my arms. He threw me on the bed and shouted about being disrespectful and slamming the door in his face. He yelled, "You'll never do that to me again!" He began to hit me. I rolled and twisted to move out from under him and get away from the blows.

"I don't know how it happened. He was angry. He held my hands together. As I twisted, trying to get him off, he began yanking down my jeans. He snarled that he would teach me who was in charge and give me what ..."

Pam choked on the knot in her throat.

"...what I had been asking for," she continued hoarsely.

She cleared her throat and murmured, "and then he raped me. I screamed and fought, but it did no good."

Pam sat with her eyes closed.

There was a long silence. Dr. James sat quietly.

"My life ended that night," she whispered.

Rory reached over and touched her hand.

"After he left my room, I lay on my bed. I wanted to die. I clenched my fists and screamed at God. I had tried so hard and fought so long, for what?

"After they were asleep, I packed a few clothes, took what money I had and left. I couldn't go to friends. I knew that no one would believe me. My father was very powerful in our town and I had no one. I knew I would never go back home. I hated him; I hated God; and I hated my mother."

Pam leaned forward and cried softly with the memory. It was no longer an ache for what had been, it was the pain and sorrow for what she had never had, a safe and loving family.

"I screamed that I would never be taken advantage of again. From then on, I decided what I would do and what I would not do to survive.

I was a fugitive. I didn't know if my parents were looking for me, if the police would be after me and so I left our town, and found my way to other cities. I met people within the homeless community. I heard their stories and observed their lives. I questioned my life and wanted many times to die.

"You know the life of the streets." It was more statement than a question.

Rory nodded.

Pam waited. Then, she spoke again.

"My life made no sense. It was a survival, existence, and for what? Others around me were the same. It seemed as if the weight of the poor, the sick, and the unhappy was increasing so rapidly that the world would soon fall into a deep pit where everything was black, ugly, and dead.

"About two years ago I felt that I was at the end. I didn't trust God; didn't trust people. But I had learned to trust a part of myself I called Shadow. It was a voice I heard within my mind. Shadow had told me whom to watch out for, where to go next, and how to find food. He had reassured me when I felt alone. At first I thought it was just ideas I had, but somehow, the voice I called Shadow felt different – stronger maybe.

"I didn't always listen. I found that when I didn't, I was sorry, I got into trouble or missed something or someone who could have helped me at the time."

Pam sighed.

"Are you getting tired?" Rory asked.

"Yes, a little."

Breathing deeply, Pam realized that she was more than a little tired.

"Actually, I am very sleepy. I wonder if we could talk again tomorrow. It has been so helpful to me, but I would like to lie down."

"I think you have covered a lot of ground tonight and, yes, tomorrow would be a good time for me. What about right after dinner?" Rory suggested.

Pam nodded as she rose. Dr. James stood and opened the door for her. She smiled.

"If you need anything tonight," Rory said, "ring the buzzer by your bed."

She nodded as she turned and walked down the hall.

He sat for a few minutes contemplating the day. First, Gerri, the young woman at the hospital and now Pam. Two young women in pain because of the actions of extremely aggressive men.

CHAPTER 12

The next morning Rory left home early. He wanted to stop by the hospital before he started his office appointments. He had called and checked on Gerri last night. The nurses said that she was still not responding. Her doctor had hoped to release her to go home today, but wanted some counseling support available to her.

Rory pushed through the hospital's front double front doors and strode down the hall to the elevator. As he rode to the third floor, he thought about this young woman. What was there about her that felt so familiar? Technically, she was not his patient, but he knew that he would be there for her. The elevator doors opened.

As he turned to walk down the hall, a voice inside his head screamed, "Get to her room, get there now!" He started to run down the hall, aware that others were looking at him; but he did not care. He rounded the corner and was surprised to see a tall, blond man coming out of Gerri's room. Their eyes met. The look in the man's eyes told Rory that something was not right. Rory felt the blow in his stomach, the old vision.

The young man ducked into the stairs and Rory sprinted into room 316.

Gerri was lying curled up in bed, her arms wrapped around her knees. Her quiet sobs muffled by the blanket. Rory slowed his pace and sat in the chair by her bed.

"I'm here," he whispered.

She made no reply and he simply sat. He touched her hands and quietly cried her pain.

Despite her self, his presence penetrated her wall. She heard his quiet sobs. She raised her eyes to his. As their eyes met, she knew that right now, in this moment, she did not want to be alone with her pain. She wanted to be in the safety of this man. Gerri reached for him and leaned into his arms. As his strength enfolded her, she knew she was home. They cried together for a time that was beyond this moment. It reached back to a woman's limp body, to loss and to grief.

Rory and Gerri held hands. Gerri told him the events of the morning; Dean's sudden appearance at her door; his threats and his assurance that he could find her no matter where she was; hatred had tinged every word.

"Gerri, there's nothing this man can do to you. There are laws and I am here. He will never hurt you again."

She cried.

He lifted their hands and gently kissed her fingers with his lips. A shock went through both of them. Why was that so natural, so familiar?

Rory cleared his throat. "I want you to listen to me." He held her eyes with his. "I am here and I am not going away. Do you hear what I am saying?"

Gerri nodded her head.

"Are you ready to talk to the police? I could call my friend, Sergeant Palmer."

"Would you stay while he is here?" she asked.

"Yes," said Rory. "I wouldn't have it any other way."

"Then, I am ready," she whispered quietly.

After staying with Gerri for the greater part of the morning as Sergeant Palmer asked questions, Rory went to his office. He was committed to her. Nothing would move him away.

When his last client left, he drove to the Center.

After eating and visiting with the staff members, he went to his office to meet with Pam. He made a quick call to assure Gerri and was ready when Pam knocked on his door.

"Come on in." he called.

She came in. Looking refreshed, she settled into his soft overstuffed chair.

"Are you ready for more?" she asked with a smile.

Rory returned her smile and nodded.

Pam shifted her body, scanning the wall as she sorted her thoughts. Then she continued her story.

"One day, about two and a half years ago, I woke to the despair of another day alone. I was at a shelter. You can't rest much in shelters. You always have to be on guard to protect your bundle, and even your life. All the night noises, snoring, nightmares, constant movements of other people make it hard to sleep. Then you have to be up at 5 in the morning and out on the streets by 6:30 with another day that is just like the one before. You panhandle or pretend to keep busy doing nothing.

"I was so discouraged that morning. I picked up my bundle and headed out the door. It wasn't just my existence that depressed me, but the craziness of what I was seeing everywhere. The threads of my life were all woven together in such an ugly picture. I asked myself, "Who put the threads together so unfairly for some and so magnificently for other? Was it God? Was it parents? Was it the system?" I walked to a spot by a freeway off ramp, a place where I could be alone.

"I didn't think God would help me, but I cried out to Shadow, "Please, please help me to understand the craziness of this life! Why has this happened to me? Why me? How can I get out of here?'

"I was angry, I was sad, I was powerless to change anything, but I couldn't go on like this.

"I sat on my bundle of possessions and cried until there were no more tears. I may even have slept. Then I sensed words from Shadow.

'Dear one, pick up your bundle and walk over to the park'

"I opened my eyes and looked around. Then I heard again, 'Walk over to the park.'

"I stood and picked up all I owned in this world and walked the seven blocks to a park.

"As I got to the edge of the grass, I heard,

'Go and sit under the large oak tree.'

"I walked to a far corner of the city park. I settled myself on the grass, leaned against the trunk of this magnificent oak and closed my eyes. Almost immediately, I felt the most glorious feelings sweep over me. It was like I was a wet canvas and a paintbrush dipped in blue watercolor spread across my head. The paint slowly moved down my body and then the next stroke came and the next. I cried. I felt a joy and love I hadn't known was possible. I kept whispering,' Thank you, thank you.'

"Then I heard, 'This is what life is about!'

"I wept. I hadn't known anything could be so wonderful. My physical body was bursting with warmth and love.

"I asked, 'How do I keep this? How do I live from this amazing place? I didn't know that this was possible.'

"I thought about some of my friends on the street. How would they act if they felt this love and safety? I let my imagination take over and I saw their life unfold like a story before my eyes. I saw them change. There was light in their eyes. Experiences of respect and opportunity came to them. Joy in living opened their mind to options they had not thought possible. With my imagination, I put other people into that space of love and warmth. The hardest one to put there was the man who had been my stepfather. The changes I saw in him were instantaneous, effortless and monumental.

"Then I wondered. Why had I not known or felt this energy before? Why are humans not allowing love and joy to be the point from which their decisions and experiences flow?

"And that is when the first of my dreams or visions come.

"I saw myself, not as I look now. I stood in front of a large gathering of men and women. My copper hair was long and flowed over my rich green cloak. I seemed to move without effort but clearly I was very anxious, on the verge of panic. Some great danger loomed. I was sharing something that had caused my concern.

"I asked Shadow what was happening.

"Shadow answered, 'This Council meeting occurred just before your first birth onto this planet many lifetimes ago. There was a plan for volunteers from more sheltered worlds to birth into human families. It was called the Joehicca mission. The intention was to wake up the consciousness of humanity from within families. You were one of those volunteers. Your worlds still held memory of Earth's plan, they had forgotten. As a result of their loss of Earth's purpose, their energy had become denser. Her inhabitants were less alive, more fearful and their mission remained unfinished.

"I said to Shadow, 'That sounds like what I see every day on the streets.'

"Shadow continued, 'Myra, a close friend of yours, was among the first volunteers to enter Earth . She realized that something was very wrong. She called to you and asked that you check out her systems. As you did, you found major problems. Circuitry had been manipulated. An overlay at the brain stem that was controlled by the Outsiders. Re-engineered body patterns that locked humanity into slave existence. And the circuitry for spiritual maturation was missing. That is what you are reporting to the Council. You realized that there was no way this mission could succeed."

"Just a moment," said Rory. "I want to think about that idea."

He sat and thought about some of his clients. He recalled those who had tried so hard. There were many with inappropriate behaviors, ways of thinking that sabotaged life. Some had stunted maturation caused by early childhood injuries; and some clients had little or no emotional responses. In treatment, one situation would be uncovered, addressed, desensitized, but it would lead to another, and then another. There seemed to be a mushrooming effect. It took daily, sometimes minute-by-minute, effort to stay focused on health. For some it was too much. Time and time again he had looked for more information; more skills to break what seemed to be impossible cycles. What if some of what he saw was caused by crippled systems within the body suit?

Rory nodded and Pam continued with Shadow's explanation.

"Shadow had more to share. He said, 'You knew that these malfunctioning systems would make it impossible for the volunteers to succeed. In these bodies, they were crippled. Your soul companion, Jerra, and some of your dearest friends were already on the Earth in those physical bodies. That is why you are so concerned.'

Pam continued, "I saw myself standing in front of that gathering and then I seemed to slip into that body. I felt as if I were literally there. I heard someone speak. I knew that it was Sela, the President of the Council.

"It was known that there was crippling in the physical suits,' she said.

"Then, why was this mission permitted?" I asked her.

"It was hoped that the energetics of the volunteers would override the malfunctions of the physical body's systems. That would have been the easier way."

"Clearly, that is not happening.

"So, we do have a back up plan. As you know, there are highly evolved volunteers to be birthed, a segment of the Joehicca. They have been named the Sihedaa and have a specific mission that is the hope of our family. One stipulation for this planet is that it be a place where individuals choose their direction.

"Another member of the Galactic Council spoke.

"The Sihedaa volunteers will be guided and watched over. Eventually, they will remember that something is wrong. As they acknowledge that fear is not a reflection of their Divinity, they will reach for answers. They will take back their life and begin making decisions that will enable them to shake off old patterns. As they demand help for themselves, they will receive help and answers. Their quest will cause a shift within the Joehicca volunteers and then the Ancient Ones.

"Until then, we will continue to stabilize the fields of energy around the Earth."

Rory thought of those clients who came to him. It was true that those who were able to admit that they had a problem and to ask for help began to find answers. Pain often forced them out of their denial, their insistence that life was okay. It was difficult to help someone who would not or could not see problems. No matter how clearly others saw the need, the person had to decide. He brought his attention back to Pam.

"Then I asked Shadow about the systems in my body. Were they correctly connected? I felt a new presence, a very loving woman. She whispered, calling me Dana, "Dana, your systems need corrections and old energies must be transformed. As in every physical body, your systems have stored the trauma that you have experienced from your first birth thousands of years ago.

"The abuse you experienced in this current lifetime has disrupted pathways in your brain and neurological systems. What has been ignored in earthly societies is that abuse and neglect, whether it is real or imagined, will cause neurological disruptions. That is true in all Earth beings.

"She continued, 'Your pain has helped you to wake up and to ask for help. It is critical that the mission you were assigned by this Council begin. Now is the time for change."

"My mission?" I asked.

"Yes. You will not stop asking questions until you restore the truth of our Galactic family. You are tenacious and courageous enough to awaken the original Earth mission and bring together the Sihedaa volunteers. We need you there. That is why you could not leave. We thank and salute you for your courage.'

"I sat on the grass and cried. There seemed to be hope for me, maybe hope for this planet. All I could think to say was, 'I'm willing!'"

In a city far from where Pam told Rory her story, Bob felt drawn by the mountains. From as far back as he could remember he had loved nature. He and Nature seemed linked at his beginning. He filled his car with camping gear and headed for a weekend by the lake.

As he drove, predictions of the planet's destruction ran through his mind. There had been many over the years. The punishment of God. Cities falling of into the sea. Mountains crushed, deserts raising, the end of life.

Love of the Earth and her beauty, reverence for her creations swelled his heart. As a child he had heard the trees. They told of beauty, of safety and of love. The songs of the backyard birds nurtured his soul. He never questioned their calming voices.

As he grew older, he heard the stories about Earth's end, its destruction followed by peace. He had accepted that this was the way life would unfold.

It wasn't until recently that he questioned the need to destroy something that was so perfect and beautiful. By then he had grown to understand the very real gifts of healing and wisdom that the Earth contains. The forests and meadows, the peaks and valleys, the plants and animals were not incidental to life. They were critical to life.

Ending wars and refusing to kill that made sense. Stopping abuse and hatred - that he would support. But ending the gifts from his mother, the Earth? That was crazy. And he began to demand a change in the plan...whatever the plan was.

As he pulled into a camping spot and wandered to the lake, the sun played hide and seek with the billowy clouds. Bob remembered the day he had first decided to act. He had gone off by himself, backpacked into a pristine meadow surrounding another lake. He was very troubled. Newspaper, TV, and even a friend at work were talking about the latest concern: the coming end of the planet.

He had stood by the lake and faced toward the sun. It seemed as through the strength from unseen forces flowed into his feet anchoring him solidly to Mother Earth and coursed upward through his outstretched arms and out his fingertips. He spun slowly in a circle, arms outstretched and cried out to the Sun, the Giver of Life.

"I do not accept the idea of Earth's end! I will not let go of my Mother, the Earth. I will not allow destruction and abuse of her creations. With whatever authority I have, I call for an end to that which is truly false and endangering, the dishonest and fear-based behaviors of mankind." The words had cried out from deep within. "That which is true and beautiful and life-enriching will be protected and maintained."

He had felt like a pole of energy, a vortex. He moved from some unknown core place and spoke words with passion. He saw a vision of the Earth lifting and lighter, cleansed and sparkling in the morning sun. He felt an overwhelming love fill his body and flow out of his hands. His heart opened and sang. He cried tears of joy and his mind opened to voices he had only sensed but had never heard clearly. From that time on, Bob knew that the Earth's choice was to be birthed into more life and love and joy. He knew and held that vision for her with all the power and strength he had.

On this weekend trip into the mountains, he felt the importance of commanding and anchoring the vision for the Planet. It was time for those on mission to wake up, to remember the original purpose for the Earth and to ignite their assigned purpose. A meditation opened for him and he followed the directions.

"Let your consciousness drift back in time. Sense the dimension of clear Light. Feel the peace, the love, the contentment and the Oneness.

"See the earth, a sphere within greater Light, totally connected to unlimited Source.

"Boundaries surround the Earth and protect the flow of clear universal energy. Nothing can taint her Divine purpose. She exists in complete harmony and love.

"All elements, earth, fire, water, air, minerals, plants, and animals are freely available to one another with honor and balance. All Earth lifetimes reflect her wholeness.

"All contrary energy has been transmuted into Light or removed to its place of origin."

With that meditation firmly broadcast, Bob sat down and let the sense of love fill and lift him.

CHAPTER 13

Pam's conversations changed Rory. Others noticed. He found himself listening to people in a different way. He looked into people's eyes. He listened for indications of joy. He watched for passions to be nurtured. And at the back of his mind was the question, "Is love of life, love of self, love of others present?"

Many worked to pay monthly bills and felt burdened. Some carried intense heaviness that left no room for feelings, period. Others were caught up in causes fueled by blame, judgment or fear. Others were busy clawing up some corporate ladder.

Whether he looked at people in his life, in his practice, on television or in newspaper articles, there seemed little evidence that joy, love and trust were the foundations for people's lives. He saw some who seemed, at times, to radiate joy, but that came and went. It did not seem to be consistent.

He was especially aware of his own feelings. He knew that he was busy, tired, frustrated, and sometimes satisfied. There was never a time during the next two days that he could identify with what Pam had described.

Now he was sitting again with her to hear more of her story.

"For a few days after my experience, I watched myself and others. Some of the craziness began to make sense. I could see the possibility that if humans were in a crippled inner state, they would act in the ways that I saw around me," Pam began.

"I tried to will myself back to feel the brush strokes of love in my body, but I could not make it come back. I wandered to the park, sat under the oak and nothing happened.

"Then the third morning, I awoke and just felt that today I could hear some more. I remember thinking, 'Shadow, please help me to know what to do.'

"This time, Shadow told me to find the group of willow trees. They were on the far side of the park, closer to the baseball field.

"I took my bundle of possessions and hurried over to that area. I sat down and thought, 'Okay, I'm ready to know more.'

"Then I remembered the law of this planet, that my request was the key. What do I want to know?' I asked myself.

"And so I started with questions.

"It is possible for the circuitry to be corrected within an individual?'

"Yes," came the answer from Shadow.

"Is the circuitry incorrect at birth?"

"'Yes, there are major disconnects and overlays within every human vehicle. It is impacted by family systems and also by individual experiences carried over from other lifetimes. These problems will show up in various ways, even in a baby. Increasingly, as the child matures, the patterns become more evident. Most problem patterns that seem to begin later, say at age eighteen or thirty, were really there all along,' my inner guide explained.

"Is it possible to have those system and circuitry shortages corrected or must an individual deal with these shortages through life?'

"'It is critical that corrections and reconnections be made,' Shadow insisted.

"Do we humans know how to correct the circuitry?" I asked.

"No. Some information is known, but not enough to complete the task. There is still much to be explained when there is someone asking for the information,' was Shadow's reply.

"Then, how can we do it?'

"'Begin with what you know and when you need more information, ask us. Don't stop asking questions. Remember your assignment,' was Shadow's advice.

And then I asked, "If we get the body suit corrected will Earth's problems end?"

"I guess Shadow has a sense of humor because I heard a faint chuckle.

" 'Well, we all wish it were that easy, but unfortunately, the problems have been around a very long time and the effects from them are crystallized through many Earth systems. But correcting the circuitry is a critical piece,' was the answer.

"Piece, you mean there is more?'

"'Oh, yes,' Shadows words came with certainty.

"Tell, me about it, I need to know as much as I can about what we are dealing with.

"I heard Shadow chuckle, 'Sounds like the Dana I know.'

"That's when the second vision opened up in my head. When the images began, I lay down under the willows and pulled my bundle to pillow my head. I worried for a minute that I would be asked by the police to move on, but that thought vanished and I watched the story unfold.

"I recognized myself. I was floating above a home; it looked like very, very long ago. The woman was pregnant. Somehow I knew I was the intended baby. She was to be my mother. She was young. The home was very meager. She was alone in the single-roomed home. It was very clean and she seemed so happy about carrying me. I could hear her singing and talking to me. Being near her I felt loved and peaceful.

"Then I was in another place. I had a feeling it was my real home. I was discussing plans for my birth; what I was to remember, others in physical bodies from this Home with whom I was to connect for this mission, how I would recognize them and more.

"I knew that I could be gone a long time. I was told that there would be difficulties, and yet I was in an environment of such love, empowerment and joy. I can't really put it into our words. I understood and accepted that this mission to the Earth would be hard, but in that space of love, there was no way I could really understand."

Pam looked at Rory, questioning her ability to explain and his ability to understand.

He nodded and seemed to comprehend.

"I guess this was a final review before my birth onto the Earth planet because I began to feel drawn back to the home and of young mother-to-be.

"This time, as I moved toward Earth, I sensed a great Light. I was not alone. Amazing love from my real home filled my heart. It was very much like the time I felt washed over like a watercolor canvas. As I was moved toward the physical sphere, I sensed what appeared to be a dense cloud. Several other – friends- were focusing in around me as I moved. Although my friends were there, the denseness began to cut off my sense of their presence."

Pam did not mention Jerra. Jerra, her deepest love and the holder of the vision. Where was he and how could she ever find him? Memory of him was her deep thread of connection to love and at times her greatest pain. She stopped her thoughts and brought the focus of her mind back to Rory.

"I cannot tell you the panic I felt as I was drawn through the cloud; the shock from Earth's density; and the pain of physical birthing into the body.

"As I relived this birth experience, I could understand why I have been angry at what I call God. Even though all of the help from the Lighter vibrational realms is available, that dense cloud of negative energy around and on the Earth made me feel cut off from them. I eventually made up the story that I had been abandoned on a dead planet. I know others have had similar feelings. Some of the people on the streets, are angry, lost and helpless. I felt like something strong and powerful had put me in situations from which I could not escape."

"And so what had you learned by then?" Rory asked.

"Well, several things," Pam replied. "But eventually I knew the bigger picture. It is more than we have talked about yet. I know it will bring up questions but just let me lay it out, okay?"

Rory nodded.

"Eventually I was shown the beginning. I learned that we, as a family, had inserted a chip into our own life flow from Source. This chip would make distorted frequencies possible. Then, because we wanted to know what these frequencies were like, we reconfigured our numerical formula. We inserted numbers that would occasionally bring in the distorted waves. These spontaneous vibrations would shift us from stable to non-stable every time they lined up. We introduced these vibrations with the intention that we would shortly end the experiment. Instead, we got stuck. Now we call the stable and non-stable frequencies love and fear. We accept them as necessary and as our nature. Not true, by the way. It was our vulnerability during the periods of instability that allowed the parasitic Outsiders to invade our family.

"I understood that the original purpose for the Earth and the mission of the Ancient Ones, after establishing a way to access the Earth's resources, was to identify anything that would diminish life or limit our abilities. This happens because of the parasitic societies.

"I learned that the Ancient Ones were well prepared. The body suits had been designed with care and worked well. As they explored the planet to discover and develop food sources and establish suitable homes, their numbers stayed few. Hidden from the parasitic monitoring, those in female suits had greater access to Mother Earth. They could design, create, and choose agendas for the good of the mission. The male bodies were to stay in resonance with the higher vibrations, our Divine nature of love, joy, self-valuing and curiosity. They retained constant contact with the teams in the unseen worlds we call spirit.

"With this activity, the males appeared to the parasitic monitoring as if nothing was being done on this new planet. All the while, the females were setting the foundations of a society able to move out from under the parasitics and rebirth into our Divine nature.

"So everything was going well.

"All that changed shortly after the activation of female's major mission, the assignment to begin discerning the presence of the evil, constricting parasitic Outsiders.

"That's when the circuitry of every physical body suit was crippled. The natural communications were overlaid with Outsider's mechanism and eventually the source for the body was shifted from our seventh Klicon region to the negative regions of the parasitic worlds.

"Along with this devastating news, I learned that there is immense help available. That there is a mission force, the Joehicca and Sihedaa, in place to correct and transform all that has held our family subjugated. Our limits are the result of crippled systems and old patterns. They do not reflect the truth. There are those on the Earth and in Spiritual realms who are committed to do whatever of integrity it takes to restore Earth and her inhabitants to the Light of Divine Wholeness that we call Love.

Gradually Eve opened her eyes. From her place on the ground, she listened. The stranger acted as if he were the master of the garden. How absurd, she thought. She looked over at Adam and he seemed to be in a trance. What was happening? She held tightly to Adam's hand but there was no reassuring response.

Eve heard snatches of words. "… you cannot taste that tree" … "not yours to experience" … "you cannot know what is good and evil."

What did he mean? She had tasted. Of course she could tell the difference. She had felt the joy, the excitement of some forms and the constrictions and shutting down of her breath at the taste of others. Even now, in this energy, when she was having a hard time staying focused, she knew this message was not good.

What was that he said? "…have to leave… earn sustenance through sweat and hard work… No longer create effortlessly…"

Eve felt a bit weak, but Adam was unresponsive, frozen in place. She reached out to hold onto him. Whatever they must face, they would do it together.

She thought that she was strong, but she was not strong enough yet for this energy. She would stay close to Adam, continue to learn from her teacher and when she was ready, she would do what was needed.

The words "…cannot know… creations through pain…" echoed in her mind as she and Adam moved away from their beautiful home.

CHAPTER 14

Rory leaned back in his chair. He closed his eyes to conjure up the feel of Gerri in his arms. She felt like home to him. He thought about the time he had spent with her and the surprise at his growing love.

The encounter with Dean in the hospital had cracked open a wound that Gerri had sealed off lifetimes ago. For some unknown reason, she felt safe enough with him to share some of her fears. He shuddered to think what would have happened had he not been there.

Home from the hospital, he knew she would need time to rebuild. Rory had seen what the normal healing course of such a traumatic experience could be. He had listened and had watched Pam very closely. The scars, cycles and patterns he would expect from traumatic experiences such as hers were not there. He knew that somehow she had managed deep healing. Her thoughts and behaviors were what some clients were beginning to reach only after many years of committed work. He wondered if Pam's insights could help Gerri to heal more deeply.

Rory had some questions for Pam. So he was ready with them when they were together in his office.

"Pam," he began, " I am very curious about the impact this information has had on your life." He paused. "I'm wondering about observable, concrete changes for the better."

Pam leaned back in the soft office chair and thought.

"Well, at first the information allowed me to look at myself, my life and past with less judgmental eyes. With the different view, some of my anger dissipated. That was a big help."

Pam was silent again before she continued. "My life took on a purpose. I was no longer just struggling to get through a day to survive another night. Asking questions of Shadow was almost like being in school. I looked forward to the stimulation I felt with the new ideas.

"As I felt less discouraged, less weighed down with anger, hope surfaced, a hope that maybe my life could change. Those were subtle things."

"Now," she paused, " what I wanted was to move out of this cycle of poverty, non-identity and non-value.

"Thanks to my new understanding of the realm of the unseen, I knew I had a lot of spiritual help and what I eventually asked Shadow was, 'How can I change my life, my physical situations?

"Because of my experience with the sense of love, I was more aware of the despondency I had often felt. I decided I no longer wanted to live in that darkness. My choice was to know the way to a life of joy and peace.'

"At first, I was constantly aware of the crisis my life had become. However, every time I felt the heaviness, which was almost all the time for a while, I would turn to Shadow. With sensitivity to the unwanted feelings or situations, I would then make specific requests that allowed those in Spirit to eliminate the cause. It was as if I were being freed from thousands and thousands of single dark strands that had woven a cocoon around me. Eventually, the peace was there about 50% of the time.

"And then Shadow and the Spiritual healers started to teach me about ways that I had created masks from fear and misunderstanding. Increasingly, I felt more powerful, able to understand that there were messages in the pain. I began to appreciate the process. Because I had a way to understand quickly, pain rarely escalated, and in fact, lessened.

"It took me a year and a half but my situation on the streets changed. With the answers from Shadow, and the basic law of this planet, free agency, I took the reins of my run-away life back into my hands. . Eventually I came here.

"I know that being led to the Center and meeting you were concrete moves that I needed at this moment to make my next life changes." Pam sat back, relieved at the telling.

"You said you had not shared this information with anyone else?" Rory commented.

"That's right. I have used myself as the guinea pig. However, I have used what I had learned for others with what I call a Spiritual healing."

"I don't really understand what that means." Rory probed.

"Well, I discovered that Shadow was not the only friend I had in the unseen worlds. I soon had a group of healers who worked with me to dissolve my dense energy as I changed my thought patterns. When I was in shelters or in food lines, the frustration, anger, and hopelessness around me were very uncomfortable. Can you imagine the emotional situation?"

"Yes, I can imagine," responded Rory.

"What I found was that instead of being numb, as I had been, I was becoming more and more sensitive to the heaviness of those vibrations.

"I asked Shadow and my teachers how I could feel more centered, even in those situation. I was told that I could ask that the energy fields of others be cleared of the negative vibrations that surround them. My guides reminded me that each individual has unseen guides who are moving with her or him through life. The guides of others would take my request and do what was needed for that individual.

"And so, based on the work that had been necessary for me, I created requests that I used for those in the lines, at the shelters or in the streets. By asking, specific actions could be taken by their guides to lift the density for them. The energy around all of us became less heavy; I called it a healing by Spirit."

"Oh, I see now," Rory, said, "the reason I am asking these questions is because I have a friend who has hit a rather big wall. I'd like to see her walk away from it more comfortably and quickly than is normally the case."

Pam closed her eyes. A shock rushed through her body and the hair on her arms stood on end.

"She was raped, wasn't she?"

"Yes," Rory remarked. "How did you know?"

"I just know. I am here because she needs me. I don't know what that means but that is what I am hearing inside."

That evening, after his talk with Pam, Rory decided to try something that she had shared with him, the power of request to the unseen world of healers. He would turn his desire that Pam help Gerri over to Spirit, those higher vibrational beings of which Pam spoke. If they thought Gerri could benefit, they could bring Pam and Gerri together.

He sat down on his bed and took off his shoes.

What was it Pam had said about free agency on this planet? We have to ask in order to get their help? What would be his request?

He started with his desires.

"I would like to be a participant in helping others heal more deeply and quickly.

"I would like to be a participant in whatever is best for Gerri's quick and gentle healing.

"I would like to heal myself more deeply."

Then he stopped to form his thoughts into a request.

"I ask that all I request be heard and accomplished. I ask to be shown what I can do. If it is best for Gerri to work with Pam, I ask that they be brought together."

Then Rory chuckled. *I sounded very much like a prayer.* He thought of Pam's guide, Shadow, and wondered who he would trust as a consistent spiritual support. His experience with spiritual matters had been growing up in a Christian church. He felt comfortable with the master teacher, Jesus Christ. He thought of the qualities that he attributed to the Master Jesus. Holding that thought, Rory spoke, "The

Sharon Riegie Maynard

qualities of my spiritual support team are love, wisdom, commitment, honesty and nobility. They work with my requests under the directions of the Master Jesus and with integrity to His qualities. I leave these requests in their hands."

CHAPTER 15

Pam knew that she ought to be sleepy but she lay awake in bed thinking. She had decided that the way to begin rebuilding was to get her high school equivalency diploma. She was apprehensive about studying after all these years, but excited at her new opportunities. The volunteers at the Center provided the network she needed and she knew she could stay there until she was able to sustain herself. Tomorrow, armed with suggestions from her new friends, she would begin. She smiled, turned and was soon fast asleep.

The next day, Pam walked the short distance to the city library. Many of the books she needed to get started were at the Center, but she felt drawn to go to the library. As she walked through the large doors, she looked around. Mothers were reading to their small children and several older people were absorbed in searching the rows of books. Off in one corner, two individuals sat next to a window. A small bundle lay by the feet of one and the other sat with a backpack between his legs. Two from the homeless population she knew and that all of their possessions were in the bag and bundle. She remembered spending time in libraries to fill her day and to find a break from life on the streets.

She gazed down at her list.

"Better get started," she thought.

Pam took her notebook and began walking toward the row of books. All three books she needed were on the shelves. Well, that wasn't too difficult, she thought, as she carried them around the last row.

Her attention was drawn to a table and chairs in an area set off by itself near a large window. She smiled to herself. That would be the perfect study area, away from distractions.

As Pam approached the table, she noticed a young woman sitting in an easy chair behind a bookshelf who seemed deep in thought, a book open in her lap.

Gerri had also gone to the city library today. She was making substantial headway. Her professors had given her options in order to catch up her missed classes and assignments. She didn't know if she could focus enough to do the work, but had decided to take this first step. She sat in an easy chair off by herself in a corner of the library.

Right now, it was not going very well. Gerri had closed her eyes and leaned back. The feelings of despair seemed to be snowballing, carrying her away. She didn't have the strength to stop them. Her mind tumbled and rolled.

Pam laid her books down on the table, sat in the chair and quietly slid under the table. She opened the first book and began to read. Something drew her attention back to the young woman. It was obvious from the energy Pam sensed around her, the woman was in pain.

Pam began mentally to direct her Spiritual friends to clear the space and to relieve the young woman's discomfort. This is what she had called a spiritual healing the other night in her conversation with Dr. James.

Suddenly, Gerri felt a shift. It was like a beam of light shinning clear and steady through a dense fog. Everywhere the beam touched, the density cleared and a sense of lightness appeared.

Gerri looked up in surprise. Her eyes met Pam's gaze. They exchanged smiles and the woman went back to her book.

"How strange," Gerri thought. "I feel so different. Puzzling."

She picked up her book to start again.

Several times during the next few hours, the apprehension started to pull her down into the density. Somehow, almost as soon as Gerri felt it, the heaviness lifted. Maybe she could handle these classes after all.

Pam smiled at the young woman as she got up to leave. There was something familiar, but Pam wasn't sure why.

CHAPTER 16

Reaching out, Pam pulled her tank top over her head and thought of the young woman at the library. She had been there every day this week. They gravitated to similar study area, comfortable with each other. Today Pam decided, I am going to stretch and start a conversation, at least get a name.

Walking to the library, Pam skipped up the steps to the large front door and entered. The air conditioning felt so good after the walk in the sun. She paused inside and looked around to see if the familiar face was there.

Yes, over in the corner at table, the woman was writing. She seemed intent.

Pam made her way to the table and sat down. Immediately she felt the troubled energy. She quieted herself; opened her book as if to read; and then called to her Spiritual friends to clear the density. She held that focus for several minutes. And then looked up.

Their eyes meet: the azure blue and the dark brown.

"Hi," Pam said. "You seem to be here about as often as I am. Are you studying for classes, too?"

Geri slowly smiled.

"Yes, I have some make-up work to do for college. This is a quiet place with everything I need. And you?"

"Oh, I'm getting ready to take the tests for my G.E.D. I was about three months short of graduating when I stopped. Now, I'm ready to move ahead."

"Good luck with that," Gerri responded and then went back to her book.

"Thanks." Pam began her study and waited for the next opening.

When the woman looked up at the clock, Pam decided it was time to risk.

"I'm new here," Pam ventured, "and I've decided it's time for me to stop being such a loner. I was going to get soup and salad at the little deli down the street. Would you like to join me? I'd love to have the company."

Gerri thought a moment.

"Why sure. I hadn't thought about eating out, but I'd like that. Let me call home and tell mom of my plans and then I'd love to join you."

"Great," Pam smiled. "By the way, my name is Pam."

"I'm Gerri. It's good to have a name to go with the face. Be right back." She gathered her books into her backpack and walked to the library's lobby to use her cell phone.

Pam had finished the chapter and gathered her things by the time Gerri returned.

"All set," said Gerri.

She lifted her backpack to her shoulder and the two walked out into the summer sun.

"You know, I have really appreciated your quieting effect." Gerri said. "This has been a very difficult time for me. I didn't know if I could do my make-up work. Somehow, you have made it easier. That may sound a bit crazy to you, but I mean it as a thank you."

"I do understand," Pam said. "I have gone through some pretty intense times myself."

They chatted as they walked the short distance to the deli.

Once inside, they found a cozy booth near a window and laid their books out of the way. They walked to the front counter and surveyed the menu, each deep in thought; How much to say? How to interact in this new situation?

Pam ordered her soup and salad and carried her coffee back to the table. Gerri finally decided on the lunch special, walked back to the table and set her number next to Pam's. She sat down and sipped her soda.

"You know it was very scary for me to decide to invite you to have lunch," offered Pam, "but I'm really glad I did. It has been hard for me to trust people. That's something in my life that I am learning to do differently."

"Bingo, another thing we have in common besides favorite study nooks," laughed Gerri. "I have had my doubts about the human race for a long time. If you learn how to do it differently, let me know."

They talked about the madness that each had observed. They talked of small things until their food came. Pam asked questions about the town and Gerri asked about Pam's plans. Through the meal they chatted comfortably and yet avoided any probing conversations.

As they finished their lunch, Gerri asked where Pam was staying. Pam hesitated. "The Center. It's been a lifesaver, really."

"You've got to be kidding! I have a friend who works there. Maybe you've met him, Dr. Rory James?"

The information sent chills through Pam's body. Rory's friend! Why, of course! This is the friend that he had mentioned. She knew now why she had felt so strongly to study for her G.E.D. at the city library. It was to meet Gerri.

CHAPTER 17

Pam sat on her bed. Her thoughts were of the day. Lately her life had been so full. She was meeting people, hearing ideas and watching events come together as if some larger-than-life hand was in charge. People were moving into her life in perfect ways. Some would call the situations coincidences. She called them miracles!

Today had certainly been that. She really wanted to help Gerri. Pam closed her eyes and called to Shadow and her team of Spiritual friends, healers and teachers.

"I see Gerri healed of this traumatic event in her life. She gives voice to her wonderful gifts in ways that enrich all of society. She is honored, respected and loved for being herself. I help in the most divine way for her. Show me how."

With that thought, Pam closed her eyes and gave way to peaceful sleep.

The next week, Pam and Gerri decided to go to a nearby park to study. As they walked Pam said, "You know, there is something quieting about being in nature. It takes you away from the rush of people. I haven't spent as much time just being quiet with trees and grass as I would have wanted."

Gerri began, "You may think it's rather strange, but I can see energy waves around the trees."

Pam looked up. "I don't think it is strange," she said. She gravitated to a mammoth oak tree and leaned back against it. "I really believe in energy. I think it's everywhere and through everything."

Gerri was surprised. "What do you mean?"

"Well, I think that all that is here in physical form are basically vibrations. Some frequencies are so fast that we cannot see them and some are so slow that they appear to be solid. Sometimes I have seen the vibrations as colors or sounds or even numbers. In a lot of my situations during the last ten years, the energy felt really heavy. Often it was a gray haze over things and even had an odor."

Gerri was amazed. She sat down on the grass at the roots of the tree. She had thought that her views were so unusual that she would live her life alone in a world no one else saw. And here Pam was putting words to much of what she had experienced.

"What's the matter?" asked Pam afraid she had, in her excitement, said too much.

"I can't believe what I am hearing. I have seen or felt those things since I was very little and no one believed me. My parents told me never to speak of them. You don't know how good it feels to hear you put words to it."

Gerri laughed from the relief.

They giggled and began to share what they had been unable to tell anyone else.

"Do you ever see…" one would begin.

"I once saw." and always there was a nod of agreement and at times laughter or tears as long held thoughts, perceptions and emotions burst. Inner walls melted away.

The sun was moving behind a cloud and the robins sang to one other when Pam shared what had happened to her that Friday so many years ago. Her tears invited Gerri's tear and quietly Gerri began telling about her rape. Pam could see the pain on Gerri's face and hear it in her voice. This was a raw sore that was only beginning to heal.

They held each other until the tears were gone.

"I am so angry and feel so powerless," sobbed Gerri. "What have you done to get past it?"

"I didn't do anything for a long time. I lived with it day and night. The rape by my stepfather and the lack of protection from my mother colored my life and my decisions until I screamed to die. I wouldn't recommend doing it that way.

"I have tried other things," continued Pam, "that seem to have really helped. They came from what I consider greater spiritual powers."

"I'd be interested in knowing," responded Gerri as she moved. "But," she began as she got to her feet. I think we had better call it a day for now. My mom will be wondering where I am. She's especially concerned since it happened. Could we get together again and talk?"

"I understand," said Pam as she stood and lifted her books. She turned to Gerri. "And, yes, I'd love to help in any way I can."

"It has been wonderful to talk with you. I can't tell you what it means to me," Gerri said as she shouldered her backpack and they walked from the park.

As they parted, Gerri took a pencil from her pocket.

"Let me give you my phone number. Give me a call. I really want to talk about how you have dealt with your pain."

Pam called Gerri the next morning.

"Hi. I thought it would be a good idea to exchange schedules. That way we can plan some time when we can talk again."

"That is a good idea. Actually, today is a free day for me. How is today for you?" Gerri responded.

"Great. What about the park again, at ten?"

"Sure, but let me pick you up."

"Okay. See you at ten." Pam hung up the phone.

When Gerri pulled up to the Center in her mom's car, Pam was waiting out front.

"I don't really know where to start," Pam said as they walked out onto the grass. I thought I would just start wherever the ideas in my head put me."

"I brought my notebook also that I could keep track of what you say," Gerri said.

"This should be interesting," laughed Pam.

They found a quiet spot and Pam began sharing her story.

Gerri was fascinated. She wrote, asked questions and occasionally stopped Pam to think about what she had said.

Pam went over what she had told Dr. James. Other information came back to her with Gerri's questions.

"I learned a lot that helped me to see life on this planet differently," Pam concluded. "It helped me to heal my pain and to take back my life. I'd like to put the information into a form that would help others."

"I'd like you to work with me." Gerri said. "After today my schedule gets pretty busy with my college projects and I'd like to go over these notes I have taken. Maybe we can get together a few weeks down the road."

"Well," said Pam, "with my studies for the G.E.D. and with your commitments, both of our schedules are pretty full. When are you projects due?"

"Some have to be in by the middle of next month," answered Gerri.

"That will give me time to think through what helped me and ask how the same can be done for you. Let's just call in the angels to show us the way and plan to get together on the 20th of the month."

July 2nd

Gerri's note: As I listened to Pam's information, I had greater understanding of the words, "Your faith has made you whole" and "Ask and ye shall receive". I had dismissed so much because of how I saw people living. Maybe we have all forgotten how to access our right to be happy and complete.

I see the results of human's vision or faith centered in lack and pain rather than their soul essence of peace and health, but I didn't now how to live differently. I had simply isolated myself.

CHAPTER 18

Pam began spending more time in the common area at the Center. She was usually alone; it was quiet and gave her space to think. She wrote and listened inwardly as she remembered what her Spiritual friends had done for her. She asked questions as to how to put the information into forms that would allow her to work with Gerri.

As the end of the second week, she went to Dr. James's office. She wanted to run the ideas past him for his feedback. He was not in when she knocked and so she left a note folded and taped to the door. Pam had written:

> Dear Dr. James:
> I met a young woman, Gerri Hall, at the library. I think she is the friend that you had mentioned to me.
> We have talked a lot already and she has asked me to help her with some of the things I know.
> If you have time, I'd like to talk with you this evening.
> Thanks, Pam

Rory came by after work. He found Pam in her room and knocked on her opened door.

"Hi, I got your note. Is now a good time to talk?"

"Sure is," Pam answered.

Pam picked up some papers and followed Rory out the door. They walked down the hall together.

"I'm guessing that Gerri Hall is the friend you mentioned to me. Am I right?" asked Pam.

"You're correct," laughed Rory. "I'm a little surprised. Your angels must be very powerful to have brought you two together so quickly."

"I know they are," Pam responded, "and look at what I had to go through to be ready to help her," she joked. "I really like Gerri. She's a warm and sensitive person."

Rory nodded his agreement and they laughed together at the magic.

Sitting in his office. Pam began. "Well, even though the goal is to heal Gerri's trauma from the rape, I know that there is an even greater purpose. That is to allow her to re-connect to her inner divinity, her spiritual energy, and access the love it produces.

"The disconnects within her body circuitry must be addressed, but I was told that it is important to start with the heaviness caused by her personal issues. That means we will address the events of this life; experiences and patterns from previous lifetimes on Earth; family tendencies; and the consequences of our particular society.

"When patterns, thoughts, feelings or behaviors from these long-ago situations appear, they make no sense. Situations seem to come from nowhere and we feel trapped, powerless to change. Mistakenly, we use control and numbing devices to dull the pain. The distorted energy vibrations are like a blanket that dulls our senses. In that state, we are in denial and out of control. Clearing the density will give her more clarity.

"The healers worked with me from my first Earth experiences forward to the present one. They did this over a period of one year. We went very carefully. Last night, they said they could do the same for Gerri over several months without a great deal of discomfort.

"We will start with extensive clearing of her energy bodies. During this work, the Divine circuitry connections will be re-established within the physical body along with the entire systems of evolutionary codes in the DNA. The spiritual communication center will also be cleared and sourced correctly."

Rory was cautious. "How will all this be done?"

"Well, they worked on me through conscious command, white light frequencies, geometric forms and their ability to transform energy. This was done while I was in quiet, meditation like state, and even sleep. I would voice a command for protection and call for total love to surround me. Then, I would make requests as they told me what was needed. In my mind I could see them and watch the energy fields changing to become less dense. I will work with them to do the same for Gerri."

Rory only partially understood what Pam was saying. That the patterns and cycles were of long standing he had no doubt. He had seen that in working with his clients over the years.

"Of course, it is up to Gerri and her parents. I would like to be there or have someone with you to watch her reaction. It's like blazing a new trail and I'm excited as well as a little hesitant. But, I cannot recommend one way or the other."

"That's understandable," said Pam. "I'll talk it over with Gerri."

Pam's notes for the processes to be used for Gerri

Triangular Angelic Grids are patterns that have been formed by Spiritual request. They enhance energy and have movement that creates vortexes through sacred geometric forms to move an individual into their original harmonic chords. A realignment to One.

TAG Matrix for Transformational Healing

The TAG Matrix creates a sacred energy field unique to the individual.

This vortex has the power to hold Sacred Space that eliminates that dense energy stored within, around and through their vibrational bodies; spiritual, mental, emotional and physical. The vortex will cause the negative patterns to transform and give permission for the TAG Spiritual teams to participate. Among other things, it is the means for activating the divine DNA, correcting the body's circuitry, nourishing and balancing the total system of chakras and re-establishing the spiritual communication center.

Realty Shift

Gerri is the one to call for new situations for her life. Her written requests will allow greater transformation of old patterns and experiences because "As a man thinketh, so is he." The affirmation process is too slow and not as effective as a process that includes the assistance of her healing team. This team approach will cause the shift to be implemented beyond the conscious mind, into the multiple vibrational worlds of the subconscious and group psyche. It will also begin a release of unwanted patterns in the mass consciousness.

The steps will be easy:

One, she writes a statement for her new choice.

Second, she will ask the team's help in energizing the pattern." Please move my consciousness and the consciousness of all in my world into this new reality." This will give them permission and command to connect cords and activate codes in all vibrational bodies that will support this choice.

Step three, "Please TAG and Transform anything that is, has or would keep me from this new reality," allows her team to look for issues and old experiences that need to be healed, transformed, removed in order for the pattern to anchor.

TAG and Transform

TAG and Transform can be used alone as a powerful healing vortex that will cause new possibilities or Gerri can use it when any discomfort appears in her life. This can be used to give the same thing as what I have called a spiritual healing.

Note to myself: As those on the Joehicca and Sihedaa mission awaken, these powerful process will be a great way for them to quickly move out of their dense states and lead the way for our planetary shift. Healthy energy will always form triangles and Triangles touching triangles form a grid of incredible strength!

Note to myself: Speak to Shadow to make sure the requests are complete and ask for whatever more I need to be shown to do this work for Gerri.

Another note to myself: Should be fun to play with the words that represents an entire package of request, like the TAG Matrix.

CHAPTER 19

It was a few more days before Pam called Gerri. She was quite excited about how the processes had come together.

"Hi, Gerri, this is Pam. How are your studies going?"

"Well, they seem to be getting easier. I have turned in one project. But, I have a lot of apprehension about the legal processes, the rape you know. It's totally senseless, I get so angry."

"Hey, whenever you need me, I'm here," Pam offered.

"Thanks. I don't know how I could do this without you and Rory. My parents, of course, have been wonderful, but they still have a hard time knowing how to help me. What have you been up to?"

Pam could hardly contain her excitement. "Well, I'm ready to do some work with you."

"Really?" Gerri's voice lifted. "When can we start? What? I mean, how do we do this?"

Gerri's voice betrayed her anticipation.

"First, we need some quiet space and time. When we find where we want to work, I'll have a team of Spiritual healers examine your energy fields. They are great at locating frequencies that are distorted, anything that is not in harmony with your harmonics. The distorted vibrations will be cleared from your various energy fields like combing tangles out of hair."

To help Gerri understand, Pam said, "Remember how you said you felt calmer when I was around, even before you knew me?"

"Yes."

"Well, several times I used a shortened version of what we will be doing. You could feel how it cleared uncomfortable energy and left you in a lighter place?" Pam asked.

"That's right. Something changed and I did feel better," Gerri acknowledged.

"So that is what we'll be doing, but more deeply. My Spiritual team suggests that we do two sessions over the next month. You will have some homework to do," Pam laughed. "After that, we'll do specific work around patterns. I suspect the rape incident will be addressed then."

"When can we get started?" Gerri asked feeling very hopeful.

"I want you to talk it over with your parents. Then all we need is a place where you can lie down with objects from nature around you to provide a steady vibrational force field.

"Rory would like to be there or have someone with us to make sure you're okay through it."

"Is it going to be dangerous?" Gerri responded with a little apprehension.

"Oh, no," laughed Pam. "But he wants you to be supported and so do I."

"You know that the places I love best are out in nature. The park is too public; maybe we could go up in one of the mountains, by the pines and lake," Gerri suggested.

"Oh, that sounds wonderful. Do you know of a place?" Pam was excited.

"Sure, how would Sunday afternoon work for you?"

"Be perfect. What time?"

"Well, if we leave by nine in the morning, we will have the best part of the day to work."

"Gerri, do you want to ask Rory, or is there someone else?"

"No. Rory is the one and, yes, I'll ask him," laughed Gerri.

"Another thing," Pam interjected." I don't want you to drive. For a short time after each session you may feel like staying in a very detached space, even nap. I want you to be free to do that and to be taken care of."

"Sounds great," Gerri giggled. "Since you don't have a car and I may want to float, Rory is the candidate for driver.

"By the way," Gerri added. "I have put my notes from our talk into my computer. I think they are accurate. I'd like you to look them over when you have time."

"Great! See you Sunday."

CHAPTER 20

What a week! Bob thought as he focused on the sharp curves of the road. The road straightened out. He needed the time with nature today. There was no way he would allow the insanity of humankind to stay with him and the beauty and healing power of these hills, trees, animals and meadows would melt the craziness. The rocks, the trees, the water, and the air were his to care for and he was passionate about them.

His thoughts reached out, "No destruction can come to this planet! Whatever it takes to stabilize our Earth, I command that it be done.

"I call for boundaries to surround my Mother, the Earth, all of her creations and all of her inhabitants to prevent any invasion. I command her healing now!"

Maybe it was only a game he played, but the words came with such urgency and clarity. There was certainly no harm done in speaking them.

He had decided to go to the same spot where he had camped two weekends ago. It had been glorious and very few people found their way up there. It felt like the top of the world. He knew exactly where he wanted to stand to reaffirm his vision for the Earth.

He'd left early hoping for some good relaxation time.

He pulled into a parking place about 10:30 a. m. He knew the perfect spot to anchor the energy of the vision. It would take a short hike to get there. Bob gathered his backpack from the back seat and looked through it. There was water, a book in case he wanted to read, paper, pen and a crystal wrapped in a square of blue velvet.

Assured that he had everything, he locked the car and started on his way.

Bob left the parking area fifteen minutes before Rory pulled into a parking place a short distance from Bob's car. Gerri opened the passenger door and swung out her legs. She breathed deeply and letting out a sigh of pleasure. "I love this place," she said.

Rory opened the trunk as Pam climbed out of the back seat with her backpack. He gathered up the blankets and a bag of food while Gerri scooped up her satchel. They all had their arms full as they set out for the spot where Pam had done the first session. Their conversations reflected the excitement they each felt. They were on an adventure, strange-new and somehow familiar and sacred.

Her Spiritual teachers had explained the work had purpose beyond relieving Gerri's pain. They had assured Pam that these processes would remove density and make corrections deeply enough for the Gegfad and Ancient Ones to activate their missions. As Pam had suspected, it was to give them a tool to begin removing enough density to allow in-depth healing; integration with their Divine self; structuring of their life according to their individual plan; and to allow the activation of their missions.

Rory, Pam and Gerri carried blankets, books and food. They walked in the direction of their spot, a sanctuary out of sight at the far end of a small valley. An awesome rocky outcropping stood guard on one side. There were pines, aspens and various grasses covering the hills. A clear, shimmering blue lake was cradled between rocks and trees on the northern end.

They stopped in the shady grove and snuggled among the trees, they went about their preparation. The magnificent rocky cliff was in full view, but little else.

Gerri spread her blanket in a place that felt right to her. Pam folded her blanket and put it on top of the food. She then arranged her pencils and paper next to Gerri's spot.

Rory took off his shoes, folded his blanket into a cushion and positioned it close to some boulders. It would cushion his back against the large rocks that served as his backrest.

When she was ready, Gerri lay down and shifted her body until she was comfortable and then closed her eyes. Pam covered her with one of the blankets. Then she moved her hands slowly above Gerri's body and spoke a silent prayer. Then she began to carefully place stones and crystals on Gerri as if creating a mosaic from some inner vision. With that done, Pam begin.

In honor of the law of Earth, Pam asked that Gerri's angels guard their work and this spot. She instructed their Spiritual guides as to those who would be allowed to help. Pam commanded boundaries that reflected Light surround them and that the Red Rock Vortex enclose to balance and protect the space. When she was assured that their requests had been heard and honored, Pam smiled, placed her hands at Gerri's head and the second session began.

Pam had scarcely begun the work at the one end of the valley when Bob finished his hike. He had back-tracked a few times to find a way to the top of this large rocky mount, but he with less difficulty then he had expected. He climbed over the last huge boulders, took a long, deep breath and stood on the mesa. He inched toward the edge. Looking out, he saw a panorama of mountains and trees that went on as far as the eye could see. Bob was awed. The view was more magnificent then he had imagined.

He stepped back, swung the backpack to the ground and took a drink from his water bottle. His hand moved inside the backpack to locate the pouch that held his crystal. Holding the crystal in his hand, he walked around the area to find the right spot. He sensed where it was, stood quietly, closed his eyes and called out,

"I call to my Mother and Father. I am here to command and re-dedicate energy to the wholeness of the planet. I call for the consciousness of all of Earth's children: the rocks, the fire, the air, the water, the animals, plants and birds from all parts of the planet to listen to my requests. I invite all Nature divas, fairies and elves to be present.

"I stand as one who has the right to call for the protection and preservation of my family. My family springs from the Light and from the Earth. This Earth, our family home, is for beauty created from Light. I demand that boundaries be positioned, maintained and strengthened to stop any invasion or distortion intent. All darkness and density must now be transmuted and the cause of the distortion must be identified and eliminated.

"As the authority, I call for all Spiritual friends with the ability to carry out this request."

He became quiet and waited. Feeling an inner lifting and swelling of his heart, Bob continued. He knew Spiritual friends were with him.

"I ask you to begin the implementation of this request on this planet."

He paused and tears flowed down his cheeks.

"I hold this crystal," Bob continued cupping his crystal in his hands, "and program it to hold this vision. I command that the vibrations of this vision be constantly broadcast.

"I command that these actions be taken now."

"I give thanks for your presence!" he acknowledged those in Spirit.

Reaching out his arms, Bob stood. Power radiated from his body as he turned slowly in every direction.

Gradually, he came back, aware of this magnificent place; the songs of birds and chatter of squirrels. This beauty must never end, he thought. Bob sat down, brought the crystal to his lips and blessed it. What next?

While listening for words from his friends in Spirit, Bob scanned the valley below him. The lake was glistening at the far end, groves of quaking aspen shimmered in the breeze and the birds sang their songs.

Off to one side, he noticed three people in a grove of trees. As he looked more closely, he realized that they were the same three he had noticed when he had last been here.

Struck by the synchronism of this second encounter, he watched them. Several times, the tall woman, moved around a blanket upon which another woman lay. Often he saw her kneel as if in prayer and scan her hands over the other's body. He was touched by the scene and knew that somehow it fit into the sacredness of his own vision.

He brought his thoughts back to his task. Should he place the crystal here, where he had re-confirmed his vision? The answer flashed in his mind, "No, move to the area by your backpack."

He moved over to the group of rocks where his backpack lay. Moving his fingers through the dirt, he dug a deep hole. Very carefully he placed the crystal in it, and gently covered the sacred spot with soil, some wild flower seeds and stones from the surrounding area.

Smiling his satisfaction, he lifted the water bottle to his lips, took a long drink and then watered the seeds and rose to climb down the boulders.

About the same time, Rory left the grove to go back to the car. Some food had been missed. He followed the trail through the meadow grasses and stopped as he noticed a tall, dark-haired man climbing over the rough boulders at the far side of the outcropping. He watched to make sure the man reached the ground safely. Rory was about 5 feet away when he saw the man's foot touch the earth, balance himself and look up.

Their eyes met and the dark haired man raised his hand in a greeting.

Rory moved closer and called out, "That was quite a climb. You must have been the one I saw at the top most of the day. I wondered how you had gotten up there."

Bob laughed. He spoke as he walked toward Rory.

"It must be the goat in me. Actually, it wasn't too difficult, just took a little determination. The sight was mind-boggling, well worth the effort," Bob responded.

"I noticed you and your friends too. It's a great place for quiet time."

"I'm on my way to the car for some food. Would you like to join us?" Rory invited. "We certainly have plenty."

Bob hesitated and then before he knew it, he was saying, "I'm about ready to leave, but I'd love to visit for a few minutes. Sure."

Bob asked questions. Rory talked. Bob wondered, what he was doing. He listened to this man. He was trained to pay attention to words and body language. People's conversations gave clues about themselves. Bob was aware that he was gathering information as he asked questions and listened. This was certainly an unusual circumstance and yet he did not feel uncomfortable.

As they got closer to the grove, the tall woman ran toward them.

"Rory," Pam called excitedly "We just saw a large bird circle and glide above us. It may have been a hawk or even an eagle. It was like a blessing."

Then she turned to the new man with Rory.

"Hi, my name is Pam," and she reached out to shake Bob's hand.

The next day Bob sat at the desk in his law office. His thoughts were miles away from his professional surroundings.

He was back on the mountain wearing a T-shirt, jeans and chatting comfortable with Rory as they walked. Pam's face came back to him.

He could see her in his mind, could see the way she moved, could hear the joy in her voice. There had been a stirring in his heart as she greeted him. He looked into her eyes and then he knew.

She was the one.

He smiled.

His life would never be the same.

Adam and Eve wandered into the desolate lands that had been allotted them by the controlling authority.

Eve had made the choice to walk into this change of plans in order to give herself more time to hone her skills.

She and Adam set about working to make a shelter and to find food. How very different this was from the ease and beauty of the garden.

Once she felt settled, she reached out to her teacher. And that was when she was discovered it. Her channels were blocked!

She reached for her inner backup only to realize that it was crippled. Frantically she surveyed the circuitry systems and one by one found that they had all been mis-wired or eliminated.

The parasitic outsiders who enslaved their family had discovered their plan! She and Adam were trapped in territory controlled by their enemies, in a crippled body suit.

What about the others?

What had she done?

How could she have been so wrong?

CHAPTER 21

Gerri called Pam at the Center.

"Pam, I'm in real trouble."

Pam heard the voice on the other end and didn't need to be told more. Her whole being responded.

"Where are you, Gerri?"

"I am at the library. I was studying. A couple of teenage boys came in. Pam, I'm so scared."

"I'll be right there."

Pam dashed off a note for Rory and dropped it on his desk. She grabbed a small blanket, her paper and pencil and sprinted out the door. Pam walked hurriedly toward the library.

She found Gerri huddled on the steps in front of the building Her back was pressed up against the small retaining wall.

Pam sat down by Gerri and took her hand.

"Gerri, I want you to remember that I have been in pain too and know how hopeless it can feel. You are not alone. I'm here for you."

They sat quietly, oblivious to the few patrons moving in and out of the building.

"Do you feel okay about walking over to the park?" Pam asked.

"Yes, I'm okay with that. Oh, Pam, I hurt so badly." Gerri's quiet sobs continued.

"I know, sweetie. I know" and Pam took Gerri's hand and lead her down the stairs.

"I left a note for Rory to pray for us," Pam added. "He will get it as soon as he gets to the Center. He loves you."

Pam kept her arm around Gerri's waist as they walked to the park.

The sun was warm and the birds were singing. Soft white clouds floated aimlessly across the sky. People were doing park things: children running on the grass; mothers playing with babies; lovers holding hands. But Gerri was not aware of any of this. She drew strength from Pam and gave herself into her friend's care.

They found a secluded area and Pam spread the blanket out to settle Gerri. She held Gerri's hands in her own.

"Gerri, remember what I told you about my pain?"

Gerri nodded.

"After the clearings lifted the density, I could see patterns more clearly. Memories began to come back. As they did so, I discovered thoughts and feelings that were very painful.

"You are feeling the pain from an old wound. It is begging to be heard and to be relieved of the hurt. Would you like to tell me what you are feeling? I am here just to listen." Then Pam sat silently.

Gerri's hands clenched tightly under Pam's. She talked and cried. Pam listened. Time was not a factor as Gerri's emotions emptied and filled and emptied again.

Then Pam sensed a shift and she asked, "Are you ready to do the next steps?"

"I am," responded Gerri.

"Okay," instructed Pam. "lay back on the blanket and I'll cover you with my shawl. As I guide you through a simple, deep relaxation exercise and then I'll ask questions. You give me whatever answers are in your mind. It will be like telling a story. Don't worry about being right, just let the words out. Okay?"

"Yes," said Gerri. Pam spread the shawl over her friend and called in her Spiritual teachers and the angels that had come for Gerri. At her request, they lifted dense vibration from the physical location and protected the space. Pam sat with her paper and pencil and began.

"Gerri, get a sense of how solidly you are supported here on the grass and on the planet. You are held in total safety and with great power and love. For this time, you can tell your physical body to simply relax.

"There are vibrations around you to nourish and refresh all parts of your physical body. It can be at peace in this field of Light.

"Focus on your breathing. Notice the ease of your breath." Pam continued until she felt the calm moving through Gerri's body.

"Now, Gerri, there is a part of yourself that is feeling great pain. I'd like to talk to that pain. When it is ready, let it say, 'I am here.'"

Pam sat quietly and watched Gerri's face, listening to her breathing.

Very soon a quiet, "I am here," came from Gerri's lips. It sounded like a young child's voice, scared and full of pain. Tears trickled out of the corner of Gerri's eyes.

Step by careful step, Pam led Gerri through the feelings to the place the pain resided in Gerri's body. Then she asked Gerri's higher consciousness to take her back to the time this pain began.

Going back as far as was necessary was like floating on a cloud.

The story Gerri saw, re-experienced and related was surprising. She told it in short, choppy sentences.

She is young, maybe sixteen years old, wearing very poor clothing. She lives with her parents, life is good. They are happy. She and her mother did cleaning and cooking type work in order to help the family survive. She sensed that this was her first lifetime on the planet.

She has been sent to the ruler's home to do some work. She doesn't like going there, she doesn't feel safe. But she wants to go because of the ruler's son. He is quite handsome.

There is a softness to Gerri's voice as she speaks of the son.

She thinks he likes her. She feels good around him. Wants to go while reluctant to be near his father. He causes her great distress.

Pam moved her gently forward in time until the emotions began to change.

Gerri, who hears her name as Shera, sees herself in the large home of the ruler. The son is watching her from a distance. Gerri knows he is there. Once in a while, she looks up. Catches his eye and smiles.

Suddenly her voice changes.

"Oh no!" sobs Gerri softly. "He does not see, but his father is coming. I'm scared. I am so scared. I can't say anything to warn him," her words choke in her throat.

"Lighten the fear, Gerri. You don't need to feel the heaviness of it. You can safely be just the story teller."

Gerri's breathing slows.

"He's yelling at his son. He should not be watching me. I'm the father's property. He owns everything. He's screaming, 'I'll show you what it means to be powerful! This is how you take whatever you want.'

"His son is trying to stop him. They're fighting.

"Oh, Oh no... the father has knocked his son to the ground and kicked him in the stomach. He's not moving.

"The father is coming for me. I can't run. I can't scream. I'm so afraid. I feel frozen."

Pam spoke gently and yet firmly, "Gerri, move ahead. Float safely to what is important for you to see next. Move forward totally surrounded and protected.

"What else is occurring?"

"His son is pulling himself up." Gerri continued. "He's screaming and crying. He's coming toward me. Now, he's holding me, rocking me."

With the next words, Gerri's voice was emotionless.

"I have been raped. I feel lifeless; maybe I'm dead."

"Tell me what did Shera decide," Pam prompted.

Gerri slowly answers Pam's question.

"Men are cruel and can't be trusted," she began. Pam sat with the quiet while Gerri seemed to think. Then Gerri continued, "Somebody owns me."

There was another long pause and when the words came, tears ran down Gerri's cheeks.

"I can't be with the one I love."

Her sobs come from a very deep place rolling through her body like the release of slow flowing lava. Gerri turned her head into the blanket. Then she added, "Life is harsh and not worth living."

She lay quietly and her breathing slowed.

"Look around you, Geri," urged Pam. "Your angels are there to help her and Shera doesn't know it. Call to them and invite them to come closer."

Pam waited.

"Oh, yes, I can see them. They're in beautiful colors of light."

"Gerri, she gave herself a message that has anchored patterns. You have been living life from those messages from that lifetime. Ask the angels what she could understand with that experience."

Gerri lay breathing softly, her eyes closed.

"They say she was trying to understand where duality, of love and fear as well as the energy of evil leads. It was critical for her to know what these energies will create on this planet. She had never experienced where duality and evil would lead when the different energies became manifested. In that situation she did."

"Gerri, ask the angels if it is necessary for her to continue in those patterns."

Again, Gerri was quiet.

"No, she now understands."

Using the Reality Shift technique, Pam helped her create a pattern for new situations and outcomes for Shera. After the young sixteen-year-old was given new understanding and greater resources, the pain dissolved. Pam continued to work with Gerri until there was a major inner shift, a dissolving.

Relaxed, Gerri dozed. Pam kept a close watch, asked questions of the Spiritual healers and angels and did what they indicated should be done for her friend.

Finally, Gerri turned, opened her eyes and reached for Pam's hand. She took a deep breath.

"Pam, you have talked about how the events of this lifetime had their beginnings eons ago. I trusted you knew because of information you had received and experiences you had had. But, I didn't fully comprehend how the past fits together to become my life now. Now, I understand. It has designed my present."

Gerri lay quiet for a time thinking of what she had just been shown. Then, she looked back into her friend's eyes and said quietly, "Pam, the father in that long-ago time was Dean, the man at the University who raped me."

"And," she continued, "Rory was the son."

Gerri paused for a minute as if to gather her strength. As tears trickled out of the corners of her eyes she continued.

"As I slept, I could hear Rory say from far back in time, 'I will be there to help you awaken.'"

Gerri breathed deeply and with a voice quivering with emotion she went on.

"And finally, finally after all these lifetimes, that is what he has done."

Both women's eyes filled with tears, the azure blue and the chocolate brown.

Pam had shared her knowledge and now the mission had begun. She smiled as she held Gerri. Then, very quietly, Pam heard Shadow's inner voice. "You now know the basics, my little one. Before long you will be shown the greater picture."

"The warning voices are around you, but many do not want to know that the seeds of pain are within us. But, now, your children will be the message givers. Will humanity care enough about their children to hear their pain, their cries for help and finally look deeply enough?"

Surprise moved Pam back to herself. What did Shadow mean?

I have a few words to add As Dana the High Priestess. I remember that first flow of words from my Spiritual friends began: "Our Dearest one..."

Those words from the spiritual world opened the door to allow me to communicate with Higher Powers. It became my source of peace and hope as I walked out of my pain and into my life. The words of my Spiritual friends have been accurate every step of the way in expanding my life.

From the beginning, when there were questions of survival, the words came. When a glorious outpouring of love redirected my life, the words came. When I was discouraged and doubtful, the words came. When I felt confused, the words were there.

I know that personal communication with Source is available for all. Spirit speaks to all of us because it is Love. The power of spiritual connection is a gift to be given to the masses, not to be held back and reserved for the few. We are in this life for a purpose and the bigger picture must be known. Why don't we ask? Why don't we hear? Why do we live in pain? Why do we doubt and fear?

Untangling the fabric of our lives takes great courage and commitment. It requires all the skill and support we can bring to the job. Reweaving the threads into new patterns is empowering

There are many of you who are being asked to remember your promise to lead the way. I share this with you from the highest place of integrity. Just as the information has come through to me, I now present it to you. It is part of a spiritual effort to help individuals understand, step out of their costumes of untruth and move back into the oneness, the Divine that we are.

Is it only a game? Maybe all of life is a game and the question is what game will save earth and her inhabitants from further distortion, pain and inner death?

I have an invitation for you:

"My Dearest, Beloved Friends:

"Join me. Hold my hand. Stop struggling by hiding your goodness and power under costumes of lack, shame and guilt.

"We are one family. Let's play in the Light together and experience our life with authenticity. It will not be the same until you are there. You are truly Divine and you always have been Divine.

"That is what I have always known and what I am now here to remind you.

"Come, Be Whole, now.

"We need you here!"

Dana

The Cries of
the Children

And the Children Shall Lead Them

We would not hear the clash of swords
Or own our part in rape.
The ghetto wars were pushed aside
By movie star escape.
The burning bed, the addict's pains
Were not our fault, you see.
The murders, lying, crimes abroad
Did not belong to me.
Disease, unbidden, stalked our land
We found someone to blame.
We hid our heads and closed our eyes
And made our bodies lame.
But now we hear our children's cries.
Our hearts would give a balm.
We look in horror at the fact,
The monster has come home!
Eventually, one by one, we must meet the enemy and admit that it is
us!

CHAPTER 22

The sun heated the sand under the park swings. Evelyn curled her toes around the warm golden grains and smiled at her three-year-old daughter, Stacy, running on the clipped green grass. Evelyn breathed in the smell of freshly cut grass as she sat and hugged her knees.

Aware of her mother, Stacy turned and waved. The distance must have seemed a kingdom away to the small child, but Evelyn knew that with a few strides she could easily have swooped up the giggling three year old and carried her off with kisses and hugs. Stacy's blue eyes sparkled and she threw her mother one kiss and then another before stretching out her arms to turn in dizzying circles that children enjoy. Her daughter's laughter brought a smile to Evelyn's lips.

As the overcast skies of a long winter gave way to the light of spring, this park, so close to their new apartment, was a godsend. The park made it easy to let Stacy soak in the glorious sun that added a little color to her cheeks and relieved Evelyn's cabin fever.

Evelyn looked around at the various groups of children. One mother held her daughter's hand. "You touch gently, like this," she was saying. A father was down on his knees loosening his son's strangle hold on his perplexed friend's leg. It looked to Evelyn as if the dad was teaching lesson number 101 in hugging, "How not to become a permanent fixture on your friend's body." Other moms and dads pushed toddlers in swings, rolled balls toward small hands, and chatted with one another, one eye monitoring their children's play. Evelyn kept Stacy in constant view, calling if the three year old ventured too far for comfort.

Stacy was so much like her father. She had his blond hair and his laughing, "devil may care," blue eyes. *I am totally loved and safe* was her attitude. Stacy was such a child of their hearts that Evelyn sometimes held her small, blond daughter a little too tightly. But today the sun was bright, the sky clear, and this park was a great place for play and rest.

Having shortly moved to their new apartment, Evelyn had noticed that the neighborhood used this area often. Older children intermingled with younger ones and older folks walked the paths nodding and smiling to the children at play. Today must be an early day from school, thought Evelyn. It was mid-morning and yet older children were here running and tumbling with one another.

Evelyn beamed as Stacy bent to examine some rocks near the teeter-totters. Evelyn closed her eyes and breathed in the fresh warm air.

Without any warning, a shot rang out. The sound echoed, repeated and again echoed.

Evelyn's eyes flew open. She jerked up. *Where's Stacy?* She bounded up, screaming and running. Voices crying, feet stumbling. Panicked mothers lying over children. More shots. Evelyn reached Stacy. Evelyn cradled her daughter, blond hair turning blood red. She was beyond hearing.

Evelyn sat moaning, holding the small body, touching the tiny hands. Her mind in shock. The blood seeped. Stacy slipping away. Time stood still. Nothing existed, not the warm sun, not the fresh grass, not the birds' songs.

For Evelyn there were only screams, Stacy's blood, and a cave where her heart had been.

Eve lay sweaty and exhausted on a birthing spot covered with grasses, moss and blood. She floated out of consciousness only to be brought back sharply with each searing pain. If she could only sleep, stay away, but that was not possible. Just let me rest, she thought, just a short rest.

Deep in the shadows of her memory she knew that this was not what had been intended. The Ancient Ones who came knew that before children came there must first be a great cleansing of evil, and then the design of a multitude of abundant gardens from the resources of Mother Earth, an anchoring from love and creation of beauty. Her creations, all manner of creations, were to have been birthed with ease into a world designed to cause the restoration of the family's Divinity in an environment of peace, plenty and love.

And here she lay, bloody and exhausted, her value squelched. She gave birth to children through great pain, with great difficulty. She brought babes into a world in which she had no voice. She had no say for their welfare, their future, their guidance. They belonged to others, to the Outsiders who took them as laborers, as warriors, as slaves and fodder.

Eve let out a scream as she was swept by the next wave of pain.

Oh god, when will it be over?

And her Ancient teacher; cursed, hobbled and alienated, wept tears to witness this immense destruction of the plan.

And through her tears she cried, Oh Great Council, when will it be over?

CHAPTER 23

Wrapped in a bathrobe, dishelved black hair, Bob opened his door and reached for the morning paper. Crisp morning air rushed in. Bob breathed the mist and freshness, smiled as he closed the door. He stood, looked out over the budding lilacs. The tulips and crocus were finally open splashing color through his yard. He smiled, breathed in the crisp morning air and stepped back inside. He loved his new morning routine. After eight years of spending hours at the office, Bob had decided to start appointments later in the morning. That made for an unhurried morning and he loved it.

He pulled the paper from its plastic bag and walked to the kitchen for a steaming cup of coffee. Balancing coffee cup in one hand and morning paper in the other, Bob lowered himself onto his couch. He sipped the steaming brew, set it on a coaster, and opened the paper.

The newspaper headlines blared out at him.

"Thirteen Year Old Shoots and Kills Friend and Three Year Old."

Bob's stomach churned.

"Wednesday, what began with clear a spring sky erupted into a nightmare of terror. Parents sharing a spring break with their children were horrified when a thirteen-year-old boy suddenly pulled a gun from his backpack and began shooting into a playground full of children and adults.

"Six shots were fired before the young boy was tackled and brought to the ground by a father. In the short, but deadly shooting spree, two children, one twelve and the other three were fatally wounded. Two others were hit by the gunfire and are still in local hospitals"

Bob's hands flew up to his forehead. He could visualize the drama.

A young mother holding her dying child. Sorrowful wails. Blood flowing. A vibrant, laughing child lay limp. Mother's tears streaming. Rocking her child, a world shattered.

And then the scuffle. Mothers shielding their children. An angry father. The boy crashing to the ground. The father's rage driving the weapon from the boy's hand, a hand too small for a weapon, an act too final.

How long before the sirens screamed and a crowd gathered? How long before covers were laid over the dying children? Did the young mother have to be torn away, hands reaching to grasp her child? The cameras flashing and videos rolling, recording for all time the anguish and despair. His heart ached. Bob felt a hollow space open inside. No wonder parents looked in on sleeping children, searched for ways to fortress them from dangers.

Absently, he moved into the bathroom and hung up his robe. He stepped out of his pajama bottoms, kicked them across the smooth tile floor, stepped in, and turned on the shower. The spray pelted his body. Warm, salty tears flowed down his face as the water from the shower stung his skin.

Bob's mind ran over the newspaper story. Why does a thirteen year old have a gun in his backpack? Why does he even have a gun? Why haven't we found answers? Do we prevent solutions? And the media? Are we after answers or numbers?

The questions came fast. He scrubbed hard. His mind clouded. Bob turned the water handle to cold, took a deep breath, and stood in the spray. This story wouldn't let go. What is happening? he asked.

At 9:30 a.m., Bob parked his car and walked briskly into his office building. As he walked through the door into this suite, Joanne, his secretary looked up with a smile that quickly dropped away. Bob was clearly not his usual self. She quietly handed him a telephone note.

Bob looked down; the note, a call from Rory. Rory was just the person who would understand, Bob thought. He took the note, totally unaware of his effect on Joanne. Without a word he went into his office and closed the door.

CHAPTER 24

Rory breathed deeply, yawned, and stretched in the swivel chair. He looked at the pictures on the walls, the lush green plants, and the new burgundy couch. Iris White had certainly transformed his office into her own. Sitting at this desk brought back memories, memories of long planning meetings, of fundraising, of nights with little sleep. It had taken determination to create his dream for a group home where individuals could rebuild their lives. His eyes caught the crystal wall clock that had replaced his bronze nautical. The clock read 2 am. He yawned, glad that he no longer did regular night shifts.

Rory unfolded his tall body, pushed away from the desk. As he opened the door the dim hall lights filtered into the office. On a basketball court Rory had moved with ease and at thirty-three his movements were still graceful. As Rory moved down the hall, he heard the soft breathing, occasional snores, and sounds of restless sleep from the bedrooms. Rory smiled. Rounding the corner, he walked into the kitchen.

He poured the last of the hot coffee and set his cup on the counter. He rinsed the pot and tipped it upside down to dry. Blowing into the cup, he sipped the hot liquid and wandered into the common living area. Rory looked at the pictures. He smiled back at happy faces, framed memories. So many people had built foundations to restart their lives here. He moved slowly from one picture to another. In the quiet, Rory sighed, a catch in his throat. He pivoted and walked back down the hall. Good hand-foot coordination kept his coffee from spilling.

Rory stopped occasionally to listen and sip his coffee as he made his way to the office. He softly closed the door, sat down on the burgundy couch, and set his mug on the coffee table. Picking up a small picture, he looked down at Pam's face. Over the past year, she had become such a part of he and Gerri's life. It was hard to remember when she was not there. Absently, Rory set the photo aside, picked up the evening paper and opened it.

His eyes widened. He looked up. Unconscious of his movements, Rory's face tensed, his eyes closed and the paper dropped to the table. Rory raked his fingers through his blond hair.

The headlines read:

"Young Boy Shot to Death by Friend as Children Played at Glacier Park"

Rory clenched his teeth. Images of a park, the sun shining, children laughing flooded his mind. Eyes asking the unanswerable, "Why?"

"Damn it," he whispered. "Damn it, damn it, damn it!"

Keep a professional distance, a voice inside reminded him.

"Professional distance, be damned! I want to change lives! My colleagues want to change lives! Violence is blowing the city apart. We work, we work and we lose again!"

He flung the paper onto the floor, stood up, and paced. "This has got to stop!" he exclaimed. Pressure squeezed Rory's throat, pain filled his heart and throbbed in his head. He beat the couch again and again and again.

Tears ran down his face. "I want to know how to do more. We try so hard," he spoke to himself, "but it's time to do more!"

Rory did not know how long he sat, letting his tears fall and his mind wander. The coffee was no longer steaming when he heard himself.

"I demand a powerful solution team for children. We are people of vision, love, and commitment. We look with open, questioning minds.

Our only agenda is passionate, healthy, safe living for children and harmony within families. We do not stop until children are safe, their voices heard! I call for this to be in place now."

The words tumbled out of his mouth. The timbre of his voice was strong, knowing, committed.

As if coming to himself, Rory shook his head and sat down at the desk. Straining to remember, he wrote what he had just heard himself say.

Rory read and re-read the words. The power of the statement touched him, the energy of the words surrounded him, and he laid his head on the desk.

With his eyes still closed, Rory reached out and picked up the phone. Taking a deep breath, he looked at the numbers and dialed.

"Hi, sweetheart," Gerri's voice was deep and slow, "what's going on this early in the morning?"

Rory glanced up at the digital desk clock, 4:30 a. m.!

"Oh, I'm sorry," he stammered, "wasn't noticing the time. I could call back later. I just wanted a short talk."

Amused, Gerri replied flirtatiously, "I'd talk with you anytime."

Rory could hear her breathing. Mentally, he saw her snuggle down in their bed and cradle the phone with the pillow. He could almost smell her early morning earthiness. He closed his eyes and breathed in her warmth. She was a balm to his soul.

Taking a breath to calm himself, he asked, "Did you read last night's paper, the shooting at Glacier Park?"

"I saw it on the news before I went to sleep." She paused. "I wondered how you would respond."

"It hit my heart," Rory confided.

"I thought it might," she said knowingly. She mentally threw her arms around this gentle man, wanting to hold him until the pain drained away.

"I was so angry," Rory continued. "I wanted to run out and scream at life and at the world and at God. It's all so senseless! I hurt with all that we are not able to do, for those we are not able to reach.

"But, Gerri, something happened. Words poured into my head, strong, determined words." He hesitated and then continued, "I'm not sure where they came from."

"Do you remember the words?" Gerri asked, her words edged with curiosity.

"I wrote them down." Rory shuffled aside the newspaper. "I'll read them to you.

"I demand a powerful solution team for children. We are people of vision, love, and commitment. We look with open, questioning minds. Our only agenda is passionate, healthy, safe living for children and harmony within families. We do not stop until children are safe, their voices heard! I call for this to be in place now."

"Rory, that is profound," Gerri whispered. "That is just what you have wanted." She paused. "What are you going to do next?"

"Well, I'm going to hold fast to that vision and let the law of attraction work. I know that there are unlimited possibilities if we just set the vision. There must be others as concerned as I am. A group with this commitment will make things change." His words were emphatic.

Gerri thought a moment.

"You may want to look around you. The people may already be attracted," Gerri responded.

"You're right," Rory said thoughtfully. "I'm going to put a call in to Bob."

"I think it's a good idea. You want to wait until his office opens?" Gerri asked rhetorically and then they both laughed.

"Thanks," said Rory.

"Thanks for what?" asked Gerri.

"For just being you. I love you," he gently replied.

CHAPTER 25

Bob dialed Rory's number and waited. Rory's receptionist Beth answered.

"Good morning, Mr. Hatcher," she said. "He told me to put you right through," she said. "Hold on just a moment." With a click Bob could hear the transfer and then Rory answered, "Good morning, Bob."

"Hi, Rory," Bob answered. He noticed that Rory's voice sounded tired.

"Did you read about the young boy at Glacier Park yesterday?" Rory asked.

"Yes, I saw it in the morning paper. It really affected me. I am so angry!" Bob was glad to have someone with whom he could share his feelings.

"Man, it did that to me too, like one hard blow to the gut. I don't know how parents feel with such craziness and danger out there. Anyway, I'm calling because I have an idea," Rory continued.

"I'm listening," Bob responded.

"For as long as I can remember, I have felt such empathy for people in pain," Rory began.

"Therefore, counseling," Bob teased.

"Oh, right." Rory gave a little laugh and then continued. "But you know I am constantly confronted with the inadequacies of our field. Maybe inadequacy isn't the right word, more like the limits," Rory was clearly upset and Bob listened carefully.

"Yes, we do make differences, but look at yesterday. And this isn't an isolated, unusual incident. It reminds me again that we have a lot of people in pain, a lot of people with hurtful ways of thinking, we name it dysfunctionality, addictive behavior, manic-depressive, new names every year. The truth is that society is not addressing its negative sides and our darkness will not go away by itself."

"I agree," responded Bob. "What ideas do you have?"

"Well, I've come up with a goal. It's really something I have wanted for a long time, but I think that now I'm ready to put my money where my mouth is."

Rory paused. He was tired. The night had been long and now tears began to constrict his throat. Rory coughed to clear them and took a deep breath. Bob waited.

"Here's my goal. I'd like to know what you think.

"I demand a powerful solution team for children. We are people of vision, love, and commitment. We look with open, questioning minds. Our only agenda is passionate, healthy, safe living for children and harmony within families. We do not stop until children are safe, their voices heard! I call for this to be in place now."

Bob thought for a moment before he spoke. "I know that the only way to achieve a goal is to make the end result visible, concrete, putting it into words. Otherwise, there is no path. No path, no open doors."

"That's what I have discovered," Rory spoke, "To tell the truth, I have been waiting for someone else to set up this goal. Then, I thought, I would jump on board. That's like waiting for someone else to solve our problems. After the shooting at Glacier, I am not willing to wait any longer." Rory paused. "Maybe setting the vision was my job all along."

Then Rory put out the invitation. "What about you? Is this something you would like to be on board with?"

Bob pondered. He felt the excitement at the possibility. Then, thoughts of doubt flashed in his mind,

'You already have a lot on your plate.

'Why don't you just give support from the sidelines?'

'What about the plans you have for Pam and your life together?'

Then he remembered the morning, the shower, the intensity, and the price others were paying because this violence continued.

Taking a deep breath that moved him to his core place, Bob knew his answer.

"I would love to be involved," he uttered. "When?"

"Great!" exclaimed Rory, his excitement released. "What about next Sunday?"

"I know a place if you want to be outside," Bob volunteered. "We could be in the spring sun, fresh air, and glorious skies."

They agreed and the date was marked on their calendars.

"I'm going to invite Gerri and Pam," Rory said.

"Just what I would have suggested," affirmed Bob. The line was quiet. Then Bob continued. "I'm looking forward to this. Thanks for asking me," he spoke sincerely. Then he hung up the phone.

Morning began. Bob felt a new enthusiasm rising because a person with a vision had touched his heart.

Three Klicons from Home

The energy within each of the twelve family groups was brilliant, vibrant, a diversity of colors. In preparation for their adventure to experience chaos, a chip that generated negative vibrations had been inserted into their life flow from Divine Home. Each group had reconfigured the codes through which the life energy moved and it had changed to include discordant frequencies. The chip and changed numerical codes assured that the plan would work. There was excitement at the chaos possibility and although no one knew what would happen, everyone was game.

The observation deck was quiet. Members of the thirteenth family group stared into the vast expanse of space. Twelve immense groups of family members waited in that space, prepared and ready to activate the experiment. Excitement crackled through the air. Everyone waiting for the moment they would shift their energy.

Ica's voice came through the silence of the deck. "Okay, the switches are on in groups one, six and nine." A pause. " They're stable, no change."

Then Sinca pointed in the opposite direction, " Now, three, five and seven have switched their chipped formula. And next to them, two, eight and ten are on board. Everything is smooth. No chaos yet."

Tenta called out, "Four, eleven and twelve have shifted over."

With the energy shifted in the twelve groups, the members of the thirteenth settled back to see what the spontaneous chaos programming would bring.

Eventually, Tenta called out, "Hey, look over there. Nine has been hit with the chaos frequency."

Followed by Ica, "And look, ten is slipping into a discordant pattern."

"Four is shifting," called out Mina.

With excitement and then concern the thirteenth group watched. Like children on a carnival ride, members within the twelve groups laughed, grew nervous and screamed out their newfound fear and thrill.

"Hey, look, eight is having a hard time rebalancing," Mina observed.

" The others are more sluggish also," Ica pointed out.

CHAPTER 26

Rory called Pam at her new office. He told her about his reaction to the shooting at Glacier Park.

"So, what I realize is that if something doesn't change, we will loss more kids to these kinds of situation." Then he read her his new goal and told her about the meeting.

"What do you say? Do you want to come on Sunday?"

Pam was excited with Rory's invitation. Her work had become about people who were looking to change their lives. She had learned to trust realities of which most were unaware and was committed to transform situations. Because of her experiences, she saw the need to incorporate new ideas and so she gladly accepted his invitation. She laid her hand on the file of a new client. She had her own reason for wanting more answers.

Sunday came. Warm, fresh colors, and gentle breezes; a perfect day for Rory's first group meeting. Bob had chosen a little known lake. He and Pam arrived early and pulled into the small empty parking lot. At first glance Bob's dark hair, muscular body, and chiseled features hid his tenderness and wisdom. His professional, logical style served his clients well, but with friends face softened and his eyes twinkled. Pam was just a hand shorter than Bob with light brown hair, curly and cropped short. Her confidence was born of street schooling and angelic training more than of diplomas and credentials. They were a couple easy with each other and private in their love.

They walked down the path toward a small lake surrounded with new grasses, buttercups, and trees in various stages of budding. There were tiny green swellings on the plum tree, the yellow buds breaking open along the St. John's Wort. The rich, deep green of glorious pines was tipped with the lime green of new growth. The birds sang from tall trees and stubby brush, filling the air with their songs. Ducks and geese were gliding over the water. Occasionally, their heads plunged deep under the water, tipping their tails skyward.

Bob and Pam walked around the lake. The nesting birds called to them from the willows. They seemed to say, "Keep moving, keep moving, keep moving."

Pam clucked. "Don't worry. We won't disturb your family. You'll be safe," she cooed like a mother hen to her baby chicks.

The sun reflected dazzling patterns off the soft ripples of the lake. The light cut a path that glittered from shore to shore. On either side of the sparkling swath, the lake remained deep blue and mysterious.

A gentle breeze moved Bob's hair. Pam smiled and playfully tousled it. Bob tipped his head as he laughed deeply. Holding hands they walked to an open area and sat down in the long grass and white meadow flowers.

Pam took off her shoes and socks, her feet soaking in the warmth of the sun. She lay down, bent her knees, and wiggled the grass with her toes. Bob leaned on his left elbow and enjoyed the smile that crept on Pam's face. Lying there she looked younger than her thirty-two years. The extra fifteen pounds that worried her looked great to him. He lowered himself to the grass and they lay side-by-side, sun on their faces and feet in the grass.

"I know from the top of my head, to my toes, to the depth of my soul that we are here to serve some greater purpose." Pam whispered.

Bob turned slightly at the sound of her voice.

"May that greater purpose come through us," he affirmed.

CHAPTER 27

Bob's directions to the lake had been what you would expect from a lawyer: clear and concise. Rory pulled his car into the space next to Bob's and turned to Gerri and asked, "Do you have any ideas for this meeting?"

She laughed. "You called the meeting and the rest of us are simply showing up." Then she became more serious. "But, isn't it amazing to have such good friends that you can say, 'I don't know what to do, let's talk,' and they come?"

Rory nodded and squeezed her hand. Turning, he opened his car door, slid out and walked around the front of the car to the passenger side. As Gerri stretched her five feet, six inches out of the car, Rory took her hand.

"Thanks to whatever brought us together," he said. "I am so in love with you!" He bent his tall frame, pushed aside the strands that had escaped her copper French braid, and gently kissed her forehead.

Tears welled up in her brown eyes. "I love you too," she whispered and snuggled her body closer to him, touched by his gentleness.

They slipped their arms around each other's waist, walked down the path and across the meadow. The breeze ruffled their hair as birds sang from perches hidden in the trees. Seeing Bob and Pam lying in the grass, they jogged toward them.

Bob and Pam sat up as Rory and Gerri approached. Soon all four were barefoot, chatting and soaking in the beauty of Mother Earth.

After a while, Rory spoke. "It's so good to be back in nature again." He lay back, relaxed and closed his eyes. Then his excitement changed, it edged toward to doubt. He breathed deeply several times before he felt the calm again.

"I really have a desire to make a major difference for kids," he continued. "I'm hoping that our combined focus will bring us some insight."

Pam spoke up, "Would you like me to lead a short meditation and prayer to prepare the space?"

"I'd like that a lot," replied Rory.

Pam jumped to her feet and tugged at Bob. "Let's all stand up and hold hands. Close your eyes," she began.

"Now, gently move your feet to open the energy paths from the soles of your feet to your energy supply deep within Mother Earth."

Pam paused as they followed her lead and moved first one foot and then another.

Rory felt an inner rhythm begin to move his body and he beat out the tempo through his feet. It seemed to wake up an ancient memory of wisdom and strength. He breathed in the fragrance of the meadow, and with each exhalation, he sent his thanks deep into the Mother. A deep connection to the earth filled him.

"We give thanks for the ever-present guidance and power that surrounds us. We appreciate the abundance of joy from deep within our Mother and the warmth and strength sent from our Father.

"We acknowledge the wisdom within our very bones, hidden from other times, gifts passed down to us, knowledge beyond human knowledge.

"We are here, claiming this sacred space of light, cleared of anything false. We put ourselves into greater hands. We move into the world in whatever way is highest and best for the children. We are ready to move beyond our circle to serve and bless. And it is so."

She paused and felt a deep gratitude for those who did indeed have information that would help them dissolve that which seemed impossible. She gave her own silent thanks for these Beings of nobility and intelligence who guarded their space.

Pam waited and thought of the folder lying on her desk. She was very aware of the need for more wisdom and deeper questioning.

Rory turned slowly. He could feel energy moving up his back and down his arms. His chest filled with love and gratitude. There was a silence as each of the four acknowledged the sacred space and their desire to serve.

"When you are ready, open your eyes and be in the beauty of this place, of this planet," Pam concluded.

As Rory opened his eyes, he saw a mother duck and her two ducklings swim toward the shore and waddle onto the grass. They were certainly a family at peace. A great benediction to our vision, he thought.

Rory sat on the grass and looked around him. There, to his left sat Pam, who had struggled with her own demons and found ways to heal deeply. Beside her was Bob, who had a passionate for Mother Earth. And then, at his right, was Gerri. Gerri, such a valuable part of his life.

He was very aware that in this circle were his dearest friends. He had invited them and they had come. He began, "You all know my inner struggles to find ways to help people who are in pain," he began. "For so long I have wanted to make deeper changes. Well, the incident last Wednesday with the thirteen-year-old boy at Glacier Park pushed me over the edge. I've noticed how our attention, like the media, rushes to a tragedy, sensationalizes, creates assumptions, 'The neighbor says…' 'Did you hear…' and then the tragedy is forgotten in the wake of the next media frenzy. It is voyeurism at its worst. I have asked myself many times, 'When are we going to construct the bigger picture or stay with one problem long enough to find solutions?' "

Rory paused. "And I notice that society's systems are never mentioned as a contributor to the problem. It's usually one "bad" person, or "unloving family" or parents who "are not attentive enough".

"What I have found," volunteered Bob, "is that there are very few malicious people. What we do have are some very complicated issues and problems weaving themselves together in ways that are unique in each family."

"I know you're right," Rory continued.

"As you all know, I have a specific purpose in asking you here today. I want to begin to really look for solutions. I would like us to share everything we have learned or experienced that may be pertinent to the violence coming to and from the children. And then I want us to be willing to go beyond what we know to bring in information from those with other experiences. I am determined that we can make a difference!"

"I don't think that we've talked about it, but we'll want to keep track of the ideas and questions, so what if I act as secretary," volunteered Gerri.

"Thanks, that will be very helpful," Rory smiled as he turned and spoke to her.

"So, are we ready to get going?" he asked the others.

"Well, I am," Pam jumped in. "But first, I would like to have you read the statement that brought all of us together. You know, the one that came to you at the Center the night of the Glacier Park shooting."

"Good idea" commented Gerri.

Rory opened a notebook he had brought with him and read.

"I demand a powerful solution team for children. We are people of vision, love, and commitment. We look with open, questioning minds. Our only agenda is passionate, healthy, safe living for children and harmony within families. We do not stop until children are safe, their voices heard! I call for this to be in place now."

"Thanks," said Pam. "I want to add my commitment to that purpose. I have a lot of ideas running in my head. Shall I just jump right in?"

"Let's make this a brainstorming session. As ideas come, whatever they are, let's just get them out. We can go back later to do left-brain editing. Does that sound okay with everyone?" asked Rory.

There was nodded agreement and then Pam opened with her ideas. "What comes to me right off is that at times everyone feels stress, anxiety, and fear. When someone feels stressed, for example, it is most likely that their behavior reflects their stress. The same thing is true with any other emotion, negative or positive. If the feelings have no healthy way of being expressed to be dissipated, they can explode into behaviors that cause pain.

"Some people recognize that what shows up in their physical world has its beginnings in their emotions or thoughts. Even knowing this many adults are not aware of what to do with cynical, stressed and fearful thoughts and positive thinking can only take them so far. Our children usually have no way to separate their emotions from others.

"Then our scientific or traditional models have no acknowledgement of information outside their training or within the world of spirit.

"Clearly, the violence and pain of our children tells us that we are not effective enough. If we had an adequate solution, problems would be diminishing and they are not.

"The mental and emotional anguish of these kids is definitely coming from somewhere. We haven't gone deeply enough to understand and address it. I guess I'm not saying anything that we don't already know." Pam concluded.

"I agree. What if we take the situation at Glacier Park as a focus," Rory suggested. "We'll pretend that its two years ago and this family have brought their son to us. What suggestions would we offer? At that time he would have been eleven years old, not interested in school, turned off, few friends, but not rocking the boat. What would we recommend?"

"I know where I would start," said Pam. "I would work with Shadow and the TAG team in energy sessions with him, with his mom, his dad, and any siblings. With the TAG process we could look into past lives, family genetics, negative programs brought in at birth that need release. There are also issues held in the greater collective psyche. The negative influences in those etheric dimensions are totally left out of traditional work.

"Next. . .", began Pam."

"Slowdown," laughed Gerri. "I'm still on "issues in the greater collective psyche…" I don't understand all that you're saying and so let me go over what I've written."

Taking a moment to finish what she had heard Pam say, Gerry said, "Does this capture it?"

"TAG sessions for past lives, family genetics and collective psyche?"

"Yes," laughed Pam." Are you ready for the next?"

"Go ahead," Geri responded, her pen poised and her eyes focused on Pam in mock attention.

"Well, next I would like professionals willing to work together with their expertise. That would include those trained for the physical body, for the emotional state, for the mental realm, and for the etheric. I feel strongly that we must be able to address the multi-dimensions of body, mind, emotion, and spirit as a unit. Now I will be quiet," she said."

"As a counselor, there are several things I would add," Rory began. "We accept that a child is the physical evidence of their parents' genetics. What most adults do not want to consider is that each child is also a result of their parents' emotional and mental states. Like genetically inherited blue eyes and blond hair, a parent's fear, abuse, hatred may be passed on genetically as well as learned. That possibility is neither taken into consideration nor factored into solutions."

"That's right," Gerri spoke up. "And what about the contribution of society to the stress, pain, and frustration of children. I have vivid memories of times when school or church were absolutely stifling to me. I remember seeing the energy fields around my classmates diminish when social situations became tense. Sometimes their life force appeared to be non-existent. Even the impact of words and music on the physical level needs to be recognized."

"Along that line, I have seen how sensitive children are to their environment," spoke Rory. "That sensitivity to energy needs to be remembered. You would know about that, Gerri. Who was there to help you develop your ability to sense and see?"

"Well," answered Gerri, "I would feel stress or anger or fear and not know that they were not my emotions. Children have to be taught to question, 'Are these my feelings? Is it mom's, dad's, or the stranger's at the door?' In other words, children will act out not only their own inner states, but also the inner states of their parents and of others around them."

Everyone sat quietly as Gerri concluded and then noted the ideas in her notebook.

"Who is the vision holder on this planet for children? Or even for the children in this country or in this state or city? We know how critical intention and vision are," said Bob. "Is there a vision being held?"

"Well," responded Rory, "on the surface we tell each other that we value our children. But, it seems to me that there are stronger and more complicated and multiple messages being bantered about like, 'Children are bothersome, let's not have any.' 'How can I get kids to buy my product?'

He paused and then continued. "Children are bad.' 'Children who ask question are trouble makers.' 'A quiet child is a good child.' "

"Unless, one day, he walks over to his backpack and pulls out a gun," interrupted Bob.

"Exactly," agreed Rory.

"What about the one that says, 'My child will be perfect.' spoke up Gerri.

"That usually means, "Be good and I will love you, be different and you are not mine," said Pam.

"Right," agreed Rory. "Also, we expect a child to be a nothing until we mold, train, teach, suggest, and approve. The concept that the parents, teachers, and authorities know everything and that the child must conform is pretty prevalent."

"Just a minute," said Gerri. "I want to write that we need vision holders and healing of old beliefs about children, family, and priorities," she continued.

Everyone paused.

"Ready?" Bob asked Gerri. She nodded her head.

"Something is missing in the equation that a child is nothing until we teach them," Bob added. "A child is not a lump of fresh clay with no previous imprints."

"I find that each individual brings into this life a big package of patterns, plans, unfinished business, hopes, and dreams for further growth. Some of what we bring in is negative. By negative I mean unresolved anger, abuse, fear, hopelessness, and revenge energy, all of which can begin manifesting very early in life. I think that it's the parents' responsibility to know that old patterns exist not only within their children, but within themselves." Of course this was from Pam.

"A big part of the dynamics is whether mom and dad have addressed and eliminated their own negative patterns. If not, they won't see a way to do it with their children. That's when the parents feel like they are the victims of this little person they call son or daughter," Rory added.

"And so I will note that to heal the child, adults must address and heal themselves," interjected Gerri.

There was a pause in their conversation. Gerri glanced over at Rory and smiled. *You have started a good thing* she wanted to say.

"You know, one thing I would love to add to any work with kids is nature adventures. It could be in the form of learning camping skills, listening to the voices of the trees, rocks, and water, tribal traditions and teachings. These are also great avenues to use Mother Earth to connect children to themselves," said Bob.

"I've used physical challenge courses with some of my clients and really liked the results," added Rory. "These physical activities seem to be very important for those who have been abused or neglected, whether the neglect and abuse was real or imagined."

Pam spoke. "Probably one reason for the benefit lies in what physical movement does for the brain. Another big factor that needs to be understood is that a baby's brain is unorganized. As the baby turns over, pulls up, creeps, crawls, and then walks, the brain creates pathways. The eyes stretch and search and all of that movement organizes information within the brain. The patterns that the child brings into the life as well as the behaviors of those around her and her early social training is what the brain accepts as foundations and automatic response. Skipping these movements can cause later learning or socialization problems. During traumatic experiences, the pathways within the brain disconnect. Some experts call these children those with 'broken brains'.

"And so activities with specific physical movements to rebalance and organize the brain as well as sessions to release cellular trauma and strong emotions would be critical pieces," concluded Pam.

"That fits with what I have observed," spoke Rory.

Then he turned to Gerri. "How are our notes coming?"

Gerri turned back several pages as the foursome smiled at their progress. Then, she went back to the last page. "I'd say that we are doing quite well," she answered Rory's question.

"But what about the nutritional and environmental aspect of the problem?" she continued. "There has been so much research done on the state of our current eating habits to show that as a nation we are malnourished. I've read that compulsive behavior and even depression can be linked to poor nutrition and environmental chemicals to emotional outbursts."

"Yes," continued Rory. "There's so much evidence to say that our food is not nourishing and our environment may be harmful. We need to add that to the list."

Bob spoke, "Here it is again. We, as a nation, claim to love our children and yet we continue to allow them to suffer rather than explore and do whatever it takes to keep them well. We are so concerned about holding on to our beliefs, safeguarding corporate profits, and dictating to other country's that we have pushed away our own children. We seem to be numb, closed to new possibilities. What seems pretty obvious is that what we have been doing up until now is not working to ensure health, love, and peace for our children."

"Well, we have a lot of valuable information here," said Gerri looking back over her notes. "Next thing to do is organize these ideas into a plan of action and then, two years down the road we would not have a murdered child on our hands."

"One thing I would like to add is that our program, whatever that may end up being, must bring permanent changes for good as we go along. And if there are not enough answers, we must be willing to go to the spiritual realm for more. Also, we need to be aware of the control and commitment to fear that exists," concluded Pam.

They sat quietly. The wind blew through the leaves on the trees. The sun had moved behind a cloud.

"What do you say that we do one more thing before we call it a day," asked Rory. "How about writing a vision for children?"

"I think it's necessary," replied Bob.

Pam and Gerri nodded their approval.

They shared and Gerri wrote.

After writing their ideas, reading the suggestions, crossing out, and rewriting, Gerri read,

"In our world children are valued, loved, and held with honor and respect. All adults who parent have maturity and nobility of character that support empowering guidance of their child's maturation. A child is given foundations of universal principles, encouragement for curiosity, support for self-responsibility, and awareness of identity. Love is the basis in an environment of safety, wisdom, and joy."

"When you look at that statement and think of the interactions within our present society, it is clear that we are an immature society of compulsive, addictive adults. You can see it in the way we fill our needs, avoid our pain, blame others for problems, remain narrow and limited in our views, and feel victimized by life. These are not the marks of spiritual, mental and emotional maturity. Each adult carries their own wounds and few knew how to heal. Is it any wonder that our offspring are crying out in panic about being so alone in this big, crazy world? I wonder if our babies are worried when they see the unhealthy situations in which they will be born. Children may be little, but they have a great sensitivity and remembrance during those early years," Bob said.

"Wow that brings up another point. There has been a definite energetic shift in the way children experience themselves and their lives. Several years ago, the energy around children being born brought a greater clarity. I have heard them referred to as Indigo children. We have to add that information to the list and factor it into our plan," spoke Pam.

Gerri wrote it down.

"Well, it is clear that the starting point for change is with a clear, strong statement of intention or we have no energy from which transformation can occur," added Rory. "We need to remember that because there is so much scattered energy on the planet relating to children, our statement must be energized regularly with powerful focus."

"Yes, and there are so many people whose intention is to control and blame that which they create and prevent healing. Also, there is a lot of individual and group energy from past anger and conflict to be dissipated," added Pam.

"I would suggest that we commit to anchor our vision with determination."

"Well I am willing. And what about transmuting the negative energy, children's pain generated through all the ages of the earth?" asked Gerri.

"That's a good point," replied Pam. "Holding the vision through meditation and prayer will not necessarily dissipate the old energies. It will anchor a new vision and may set up a clash between the old and the new. We have to include the intent to release the old."

"You're right," Gerri agreed. "My experience taught me that clearing old energy of pain is a critical part of peace. Here's where having access to the unseen will be invaluable."

"Absolutely," Bob spoke up. "Here's another idea. Remember the day I met all of you? I had been told to bury a programmed crystal. What about charging some crystals with our vision, burying them, and calling to all the crystals on the planet through the diva hierarchy to disseminate the vision around the planet?"

"That's a brilliant idea, Bob," said Rory. "Could you get the crystals?"

"You bet. I'll charge them with the vision and then we can bury them in spots that Spirit shows," replied Bob.

"Wow," explained Rory, "I think we've done enough for today. Let's stop and just enjoy this great place."

"Just one more thing I feel we need to remember," spoke up Pam. The others looked up and waited.

"By universal law, unseen energy slows until it to manifest in physical form. So, the pain and violence of children has its roots in unseen energy. That energy of pain, fear, anger will continue to manifest until those roots are totally transformed. That means we can expect greater violence until the core of negativity is released."

The gentle breeze rippled the pond as they contemplated the impact of her statement.

"Well," said Rory solemnly, "I am ready to go deeper." The others nodded their agreement.

Bob grabbed Pam's hand. "Let's go for a walk. I'd like to stretch my legs."

Pam smiled as he pulled her to her feet. "Whoa, what about shoes," she halted him.

"Let's just carry them. There's a great little beach by that end of the pond and you'll want to scrunch your toes in the sand," Bob said with a smile.

Later that night Rory snuggled Gerri close. She fit so comfortably with her back against him. He was too energized to sleep. He held her close and watched the stars through the window of their new home.

"It's always so good to be with Bob and Pam," Gerri's words brought him back from some far away place.

"Hmmm," he responded. "I wonder when he's going to ask her to marry him."

"Or, she ask him," laughed Gerri. "That would be just as likely. They really are a great couple."

"So are we," he said as he nibbled her ear.

They lay in silence, holding hands, heart touching heart, with no need for words.

"I'm really excited to put together a plan from our conversation today," said Rory.

Gerri agreed as she turned and reaching up softly touched her finger to his lips. Their eyes met and they held each other closer.

"Sometimes our bodies get in the way," said Gerri. "I'd like to melt right into you." She felt like one body was too confining a space to hold all of her joy! She closed her eyes and breathed in the love she felt.

I am so happy, so content, so lucky, she thought. Her coming together with Rory demanded a celebration and the continuance of life. Their souls had called out to invite a new life to them. Their desire for a baby was a deep part of their marriage. Whether she had known the moment she had conceived or only imagined it didn't really matter. This new baby growing inside of her body expressed their love. Gerri knew that this was the moment to tell Rory.

Gerri rolled over and kissed his face. "My love," she whispered. "I have something to tell you. It is a bit early and still…" Rory brushed her hair and kissed her forehead. Tears welled up in Gerri's eyes. She brought his hand to her lips and nibbled his fingertips and shared the news, "Honey, you're going to be a dad."

Rory sat up and looked in her eyes. To be a parent, a father. He was thrilled. Then Rory laid his head on Gerri's abdomen. There were no sounds, no movements that Rory could sense and yet he was a part of this new life. He ached to reach out, to connect to the soul of their child. He quietly whispered, "I love you, little one. I am here for you. I will always be here to kiss bruised knees and heal old wounds. I know you bring pain to heal and joy to experience. I promise to give everything I have to help you do that."

Gerri reached down and stroked Rory's hair. What a great dad he will be, she thought. He's so loving, and gentle and clear. She listened to the quiet sounds of his talk with their child. She could not discern words, but the sounds wove a web of love around her. A sense of reverence surrounded them, a physical testament to the ability to co-create life. She closed her eyes and slept.

The ninth family group put their strongest members around the perimeter to create boundaries. They were able to hold their space as long as their energy was stable but when chaos hit, they could not maintain balance and the Outsiders easily pushed in.

Those in the sixth group decided to turn down their Light to appear dead. Although it limited possibilities, the Outsiders were attracted in droves when they were vibrant. With the Outsiders swarming through their midst, possibilities could not be utilized anyway.

The third group decided to escalate the chaos energy, thinking it would be seen as a signal of distress. Hopefully, families outside their own would realize they needed help. For eons they functioned on little Light, breathing just enough to preserve life.

As the family's vibrational frequencies slowed down and they became heavier and heavier, battles occurred, there were injuries, many members were captured, and were forced into contracts that made the family subservient. The fullness of their original agenda was a memory and for some only a misty thought.

Over the eons, curiosity, adventure, hope and excitement were replaced with darker experiences and thoughts; hopeless, hard work, difficult decisions, God has abandoned me, I'm dying.

CHAPTER 28

Rory opened the door before Pam had a chance to knock. They both laughed at her surprise. He stood in the frame as the door to their apartment swung open.

"Come on in," he laughed as he reached for her hand. "I saw you coming up the path. I guess I was a little quick," Rory laughed. "Gerri is in the kitchen fixing something to drink."

He turned back to the doorway as Bob came up the path. "Hi, Bob. Thanks for coming over. How was the drive?"

"Actually, quite easy today," Bob responded. "I decided to leave work early. We've had a great afternoon."

The two men followed Pam to the kitchen. Gerri met them with tall glasses of freshly squeezed lemonade over ice. They all sat in the living room while they drank, talked, and relaxed. Rory looked at Gerri. Was now a good time to break the news, his eyes asked? She smiled back.

"You know, you two are our dearest friends," began Gerri. "We're so glad that you're in our lives."

She walked over and sat on the stool by Rory.

"We have some news we want to share with you before we start on the children's project," Rory continued.

"Don't say another word. Let me guess," spoke up Pam. She stood and hummed softly, pretending to explore the energy around them with her hands.

Bob smiled at her antics. Rory and Gerri snuggled closer as if by combining their energy she would get the message.

She knelt down in front of them and took their hands,

"It seems as if there is a new one on the way," she proclaimed.

"Wow, you are good!" joked Rory. "And what do you think our new one will be, boy or girl?"

"No, no," exclaimed Gerri, jumping up. "That's our surprise."

Pam hugged first Gerri and then Rory.

"I am so happy for you! Does this mean that I will be an aunt?" she asked.

"Of course," returned Gerri. "Isn't it just wonderful? We are so happy. I have had a hard time not just blurting it out."

Bob joined the merriment, first shaking Rory's hand and then hugging Gerri.

"This is such a big step," he said. "When's the little one due?"

"As close as we can tell, it will be the last part of January. Maybe a little Aquarian babe," replied Gerri. "We're really happy," she said squeezing Rory's hand.

Bob looked at Pam and smiled. What wonderful news, his eyes said. The love and joy fairly danced around the room. He took a drink of his lemonade with a satisfied look on his face.

Bob and Rory grinned at each other.

"Oh, what the heck," laughed Rory.

"Group hug." All four friends gathered each other in a circle and laughed in celebration of life, love, and of each other.

CHAPTER 29

Bob sat by Pam's side as they dangled their feet in the water. Pam was unusually quiet today. Bob sat silently knowing that her attention was in another world.

He watched the grasses in the meadow beyond the stream. It was aglow with violet mountain lupine and yellow sulfur flowers. The sun was bright, the sky clear. The breeze caught the cool of the water.

He lay on his back, his mind drifting with the clouds. Time slipped away and even Pam's presence faded. He thought of Todd Ledbecker, the young boy from Glacier Park. Evidently Todd's behavior had been disturbing from a very young age and his family had looked for answers. Their religious leaders suggested more love and stronger moral guidelines. Social counselors talked of environment, family counseling, and prescribed drugs. Over the years they were always walking on eggshells, waiting for the next shoe to drop. And then, the biggest shoe imaginable fell at Glacier Park.

Questions filled his mind. Questions he would never be able to pursue or explore in court, but questions that he wanted to ask. He felt a slight stirring and opened his eyes. Pam was looking around. She leaned over and kissed him lightly.

"Beautiful, isn't it?" she asked.

"Yes, and so are you," he replied as he gazed into her beautiful azure eyes.

Pam smiled and then scanned the horizon.

"You know, when I am in nature, I simply relax and become harmony," Bob spoke.

"Well, there are few families who have nature incorporated into their lives. Alot of shoulds, dissatisfactions, busyness, but little or no time for sitting still. Can you imagine society's view of daily rock sitting or hourly river dipping or even regular tree hugging?" Pam smiled.

Bob reached over and tilted Pam's head up and kissed her lips. She pulled him toward her and kissed him back desperately. He held her and felt her tight body and was surprised.

"Hey, what's the mater," he asked and she burrowed her head into his chest.

"There's more to our situation here then we have known," Pam offered.

Bob was confused. "I don't understand," he responded, holding her tightly. "You mean you and me?"

"Yes and no," Pam said and continued.

"I had a session with a new client last Thursday. From the time she had called for an appointment, I knew there would be something unusual. As I made out the folder and laid it on my desk, I heard Shadow say, 'This one will open doors for you' and I didn't know if I wanted more doors to open."

Bob sat quietly and listened.

"I had known that she had early childhood issues, that is not unusual at all."

Pam was silent, her eyes closed and she rearranged herself in his arms.

"As I worked with her energy fields, did the regular work on her chakras, you know upgrading various systems, there was a presence that appeared in the room, a very dark, evil presence."

Pam shivered and continued. "He said, 'We don't want you here. She is ours!'

Now Bob shifted.

"Don't worry," Pam assured him. "I immediately turned to Shadow.

"He's wrong, correct? Goodness and Light have power here."

"Then Shadow told me that I was to listen. There was something that I needed to hear.

'We, meaning our entire Galactic family, including those in human body suites, are owned and have been for a very, very long time. We function with a degree of flexibility but only at the whim of the parasitic invaders.'"

Bob was aghast. "Wait a minute. What about our right to choose, to determine our life? Are you sure?"

Pam pulled away to look into his eyes. "I am sure. We have been owned, crippled, feed half-truths and wondered what was wrong with us when we couldn't make our lives work or bring our world to peace.

"The more I sit with the information, the more I see there is truth."

"What about your client?" Bob wanted to know.

Pam settled back against him and breathed deeply.

"Well, as much as I thought that my experience was painful, hers was a thousands times worse. She had been born to parents who acted under the direct influence of these parasitic outsiders and she was abused in evil ways. Consequently, her vulnerability from lack of solid boundaries or self worth had allowed energetic parasitics to latch onto her including the one who directly approached me. These parasitics do not want me here because I lead the mission to cause their removal."

Now Bob was a bit alarmed. He sat and his mind reeled. This was bizarre, he thought, not logical. And yet, he had experienced the impact of her work. Her ability to change the unseen in ways he did not fully understand, but, ownership? evil forces?

Sensing his struggle Pam reached for his hand and squeezed.

"Don't worry. This is not about a battle. It is about knowing enough of our collective history to get rid of their ownership and releasing the subjugating energies. By knowing about these beings whose agenda is to use other's energy we can take action.

"I can trace the fields upstream, beyond the abuse in her early childhood, what might normally make sense as the reason for her totally dysfunctional life, and go where others have not gone. That is the only way to lay new foundations for her and our Greater family. Without that deeper release, life will continue to be limited.

"Do you understand?"

"Yes," Bob said.

"So, I went upstream, and discovered that we, meaning our Galactic family, did this to ourselves. Unknowingly we began our own downfall and eventual entrapment. So, since we had the power to cause this mess, we have the power to correct it."

"And your client?"

"Wow, what a difference. I was able to create boundaries to keep the invaders out of her space which gave her immediate relief. She will be coming regularly until we have her fields totally restored and upgraded.

"But the ramification for others is what I am sitting with. This is just the beginning and I have a sense that it will lead to more answers for the children."

"I have some questions," Bob ventured.

"What about?" Pam responded.

"Well, you know the young boy at Glacier Park?"

"Yes," replied Pam.

"Do you suppose that there might have been some outside influence in his case?"

"Well, this is something new that I have not known about before nor have I done in-depth asking in his case."

"Would you be willing to look at the situation and see what we can discover about him and this situation?"

"Sure. When would you like to do it?"

"What about now?" Bob said.

"I knew you would say that," Pam giggled. "I'm as curious as you are. Actually, having you here with your own questions will help me consider things that otherwise I may not think of. But, I'd really like to move to another spot," Pam continued. "That place in the little grove of pines would be perfect."

Bob pulled Pam to her feet and they gathered up their shoes and backpacks. Bob reached for Pam's free hand as they strolled through the grass and carefully stepped around some thistles.

The enclosed grove proved a beautiful space. Pam opened her backpack to retrieve her ever present stones, pendulum, and notebook.

They spend the next two hours discussing and asking questions of Pam's spiritual teachers. Bob watched Pam as she meditated, listened, and wrote. He had been a careful observer in pursuing this relationship. He had liked all that he had seen so far. He saw a glow throughout her being, a twinkle in her eyes, and his heart sang in response. He was so comfortable in her presence, so trusting of her integrity. This woman was the one he had seen and been waiting for.

By the end of the day, they had answers that gave them a new understanding with which to view violence in children, and Bob had seen the final piece that convinced him that Pam was all he had wanted. His love for her had anchored into his heart.

Pam chatted as they gathered their things. Holding hands, they walked to his car and Bob felt elated.

CHAPTER 30

Gerri and Rory had asked Pam to work with them in preparing for their new baby. It seemed ironic that just when Rory had committed to follow his desire to make a real difference in the lives of children and families, he and Gerri discovered their own family was beginning. The work for children took on greater significance with their own impending parenthood.

What tendencies, old injuries, and sabotaging patterns could be part of the genetic package that would be passed down to this little one? What family traits and unresolved patterns were lying dormant? And what were the plans that this little one had laid regarding the negativity and the new dreams?

They were aware that decorating the nursery with bright colors of yellow, blue, and red and whimsical animal designs was a small part of preparing a space for their child. It was the physical piece. Additionally they wanted to make deeper preparations.

They drove to Pam's clinic, excited to be including spiritual transformation for their child.

The warm air blew through the passenger window onto Gerri's face. As she leaned back, relaxed, content, Rory thought he had never seen anyone more beautiful. He turned the corner and pulled up in front of Pam's office.

In the past it had been a family home. Pam and Bob had spent hours scraping, patching and painting. Now it stood in shades of light green with vibrant forest green trim. A rich rust color accented the windows, doors, and front porch. The flowers Pam had planted transformed the front yard into a virtual rainbow of colors. A new brick walk lead to the stairs and the large covered porch. Pam's logo and her office hours were painted on what had once been a family's window to the world. Rory and Gerri opened the door and walked in. A tiny bell sounded to notify Pam of their presence.

She was waiting. They hugged in greeting and then Pam ushered them into a small room. A large, framed picture hung on one wall, with smaller pictures sprinkled around it. Against the wall by the door was a tall bookcase with books, stones, shells, and pinecones. There were several comfortable chairs. Pam's creativity and warmth filled this room. Pam motioned for them to be seated.

"Would you like something to drink?" she asked. Rory noticed by her manner that she was wearing her professional hat.

Rory and Gerri looked at each other.

Rory spoke, "No, we just finished lunch, so we're okay."

"Great," said Pam. "Let's get right down to business. Now, you both know that we are here on a joint adventure. You are pretty much aware of the principles for my work," she laughed. "So, let's start with what you desire from our time together. What do you want to gain?"

Gerri began, "Well, we believe that each soul comes into life with its own unique plan and part of that plan is to address some shadow patterns. We'd like to transform as much of our own and of our baby's negative patterns as we can."

"You know that much of the pain I see in my practice appears to be a result of childhood injuries or neglect. Using traditional methods of addressing the problems takes many years. I see clients whose lives are consumed with constant attention to old wounds. We really want something better for our child," added Rory.

Then he continued. "Since working with you, I see that problems go back lifetimes or even beyond into the greater unconscious group psyche. Having seen the healing power that TAG adds, we want greater clarity for our baby. Especially, we want to make sure that the DNA codes, the circuitry system and wiring are corrected."

"Sounds great to me," Pam said and then continued, "Souls coming into earth life at this time have no need to live out the patterns of pain and abuse, but, on a soul level they carry patterns that must be acknowledged and released, some call it karma. Even though the distorted trauma and fear-based energy patterns your child created, lived, or inherited are his to resolve, you can act as surrogates to begin corrections before birth. It's possible to change as many as the child's Higher Self allows. Corrections in the DNA and wiring is definitely something that will be done. That crippling need not remain in any of our children. What better place to eliminate them than in the womb?"

"That's what we want," said Rory.

"Another valuable gift will be to create possibilities for him with the Reality Shift." Pam looked up, surprised at her word slip as to the sex of their baby.

"Whoa, that was interesting," she laughed.

"Well, we both think it's a boy," smiled Gerri. "Just feels right for some reason."

"Let's just say *he* then if that's okay with you two," said Pam. "It's certainly better than saying it or him/her," and they all laughed.

"We're fine with that," said Rory looking at Gerri.

"So, the Reality Shifts will play a major role in your preparation work for him, for you, and for your home as an environment." Pam was moving them right along.

"As you define and clarify your way of relating to each other, to children, and to the larger world, your energy can attract a soul that is ready for what you offer. Instead of just inviting in any soul, you invite with greater clarity. He will be able to decide if your home, lifestyle and intentions give the best environment for what he needs to accomplish."

Gerri and Rory were holding hands as Pam talked.

Their excitement was apparent as they caressed fingertips and squeezed each other's hands.

"First I will tell you the program. We will create a space of neutrality from which a new picture of parenthood can emerge. From that we'll watch for actions steps as the manifestation unfolds. Does that sound good to you?" Pam asked.

"Great," said Rory and Gerri nodded her agreement.

"All right, here is the plan," Pam said as she slid a folder toward each of them.

Rory and Gerri looked at the outline in Pam's workbook.

Rory read from the top. The assignments began,

1. Identify what you, as a parent, want to offer your child.

2. Contemplate and write how you view your Mom and Dad. Also, how they view you.

3. Why do want to have a child?

4. What qualities do you want to exhibit as a partner? As a parent?

5. Describe the environment you want in your home.

He scanned the rest of the outline, smiling as he read.

"Wow, that is quite an in-depth process," Rory volunteered. "This should set us in good stead for being parents."

"Well, I tried to think of everything," laughed Pam. "So, let's get started," she said as she pushed two workbooks and pens toward them. "Open to page 1.

"You have the whole office and garden to yourselves. The pages are pretty self-explanatory. I want you to follow each page. You will be describing the type of parent you want to be, the type of home you will create, and even talk about your fears, doubts, and family patterns: both healthy and non-healthy, it's important that you not sugar-coat.

"You'll be doing this initial work alone. In about an hour we'll come together and go to the next step. Can you think of any questions before I send you out?" she asked.

"I don't have any," volunteered Rory.

"No, I'm fine, too," spoke Gerri.

"Great. I'll be in the office, so feel free to wander in if something comes up that you don't understand, and I'll see you back here about three o'clock."

She hugged each of them and sent them on their way.

Pam smiled as she sat down at her desk. It was such fun to work with new parents, whether before conception, during pregnancy, or after the baby arrived. This was a new part of the TAG work, but so powerful. Although she appeared to be uninvolved, Pam was constantly holding a secured space of sacred energy within which Rory and Gerri could work.

Pam had put on some soft music. Periodically, she wandered out to check on Rory and Gerri. At first, they moved from place to place. Then Gerri found a spot in the back garden. She was now sitting on the grass, bare feet with her shoes lined up neatly beside her. Pam noticed that she shifted from sitting to lying and then back to sitting.

Rory, deep in thought, began at the table in the meeting room and then carried his notebook to a corner bench down the hall from the main door. At times he sat rather still with his eyes closed before he wrote.

She felt great reverence as these two searched their hearts and souls for purpose and clarity. A journey of love had begun and she knew that they fully intended to walk the path with maturity, honor, and integrity.

Shortly before 2:30, Gerri knocked softly on the doorframe to Pam's office.

"I have a question," she said.

"Hi, Gerri. What is it?"

"Well, on the section about family patterns, I wondered about my old pattern of distrusting men and the experience of being raped by Dean. Should I list that even though I feel complete with it?"

"Yes, list anything you have noticed. We want to get as clear as possible. Better to heal too much than too little. If we assume it's complete, we may miss patterns that would lie unseen and distort the new that we are allowing."

"Okay," replied Gerri and went out to finish her assignment.

At three o'clock, Pam found Gerri in the garden and Rory on the front porch.

"Are you ready to come inside?" she asked. They each nodded. Rory jotted down a few more notes, and then walked inside.

"That was quite an exercise," said Rory. "It gave me the opportunity to think deeply about myself, my purpose in being a dad, and what I want to have in place for my son. I really liked the process."

"Well, we're just beginning," said Pam, "and I'm glad you took the assignment seriously."

"How could you not?" asked Gerri. "This is a sacred journey."

"I think so," said Pam.

"Now, you will share what you have written. We'll go question by question. While one person is sharing, the other is to listen, be present, and really feel the impact of the words.

"Remember there is no wrong or right this is just sharing who you are and what you're offering this new family dynamic."

"Let's start with you, Rory," Pam said. "What came up for you about your desire to be a dad?"

For the next hour they were lost in a world of love, of dreams, of possibilities.

CHAPTER 31

The sun was just beginning to set as Bob drove across the desert. Dust swirled behind the car. Bob breathed in the air fragrant with the hint of rain. The familiar bumps were enough to keep him alert as he thought of this evening with Pam. After seven months of traveling this shortcut to her house, Bob could easily anticipate each bend in the road. Another half hour and he would be on the paved highway just ten minutes west of her home.

His thoughts roamed over the plans he had for the weekend. Rory and Gerri were always happy to put him up, but this time he had reserved a room at the Hyatt. There was a great band scheduled there. He wanted to have an elegant evening, a beautiful setting for his proposal to Pam.

His heart filled at the thought of her. He had loved her from the moment he had seen her walking toward him, her movements were so familiar to him, like watching an old friend. Her face shone with vitality, but it was her eyes that spoke to him. Words to an old song ran through his mind, "When I touch you like this and you look at me like that, it's all coming back to me now." That is how it had been for him.

He had walked into the relationship with Pam with carefully planned steps. The first three months he had approached their time together like a lawyer, a professional integrator. He watched as they interacted. He noticed her poise, her compassion, her attentiveness, and her conversations. Despite the draw of his heart and yes, his body, he stood back and made himself go slow. Each encounter showed him the way she led her life, the words she used, the thoughts she expressed, the dreams she had. As she shared her pain, her hurts, and her dreams, Bob had listened. How she had responded to the pain, whom she had turned to for help, and whom she had blamed. All were important clues to him as to her character. He had asked questions that were designed to learn more. The possibility of a life with her seemed too glorious to approach without thoughtful and respectful evaluation. He did as much with those he hired in his office. To do less with a possible mate seemed ludicrous. He loved what he had seen.

Time had slipped by and suddenly the red light for the main highway loomed ahead. Bob slowed his car and stopped at the intersection. The highway traffic was sparse at this time of the afternoon. A few minutes and the light changed.

He turned the car left toward the city. He felt excitement and anticipation at the weekend plans. Although he and Pam had talked of building a life together, Bob had kept his proposal plans secret or at least he hoped they were. A deep connection existed between them that made keeping secrets difficult.

Diving on the smooth paved highway Bob drove past the road to Pam's home and on into the city. Just beyond the center of town, he pulled into the space reserved for check-in at the elegant Hyatt. Climbing out of his car, he walked to the main door.

It opened into a large area where deep forest green and soft blues bid a warm welcome. A rock fireplace blazed despite late spring warmth and cast a golden hue on the brass fixtures. Beautiful fresh flower arrangements were everywhere. Like shifting gears, Bob took several deep breaths to let go of the drive and walked to the check in counter.

"Can I help you?" the desk clerk asked and with friendly chatter, information, signature, and room key were exchanged.

"Enjoy your stay, Mr. Hatcher. The continental breakfast is served in our Southwest room from 7:30 a.m. until 10. If you need anything, just ring the front desk."

Bob smiled his thanks, tucked his card and wallet back into his jacket pocket and pushed open the front doors.

As he put his car in reverse, he spotted a familiar figure in the grocery store parking lot across the street. He watched carefully. Yes, he was sure that was Gerri. Before he could decide whether to drive over to say hi, Gerri drove off.

"I'll just move my car to a better spot and find my room. Anyway, this weekend is just for Pam and I," Bob thought as he watched Gerri drive away. Bob made a mental note to call Rory and tell him that he almost had enough programmed crystals for the children's project. He would call him on Monday.

CHAPTER 32

Bob held Pam close. Her head lay on his shoulder. The music surrounded them, creating a world their own as they danced.

Pam lifted her eyes to his. The intensity of his feelings became too much and Bob gently nestled her head close to his chin. He rested his hand on her head as they moved to the music.

Lost in their own world, they touched and caressed each other in gentle, powerful ways. Pam's delicate fingers traced circles in Bob's palm. She stroked his cheek and neck and then reached up to lightly brush his lips with her fingertips.

Bob drew her closer to him and playfully nibbled her ear. They both laughed. Their laughter softened the passion of their desires and they pulled apart in an improvised step.

"Do you know how much I love you?" Bob whispered in Pam's ear as she came close.

"Do we just catch the love and toss it back and forth?" asked Pam. "I feel a well inside when we're together that just bubbles up. If it didn't spill out, I would burst," she whispered.

The ballroom at the Hyatt was especially beautiful tonight. The large picture windows opened to an astounding view of the small Northwest bay. In the gathering dusk and low glow of the outside lights, Bob could see the waves rolling and gently crashing on the beach. There was a wind bending the trees on a small island that lay to the north of the bay. The island was home to two pine trees, some low shrubs and tall grasses. Birds glided on the air currents of the coming night. Yes, he thought, this was a good place to propose.

"I feel so safe around you," continued Pam.

"I guess that's what love does, it provides space to be yourself, with your ideas and your pain," Bob whispered.

"Actually, for me, the word love isn't enough for what I feel for you," he spoke. "I could say that I respect you, I honor you, I delight in you because I love you, but the truth is that I have listened to your dreams and fears, and have seen how you lead your life. That is why I love you."

He drew her closer. She laid her head against his neck. The music ended. Bob and Pam walked hand in hand to their table by the large windows. Redwood tables and chairs filled the outside deck. The roof extended the full length of the deck and flower baskets hung everywhere. White, pink, and yellow flowers created an overhead garden spilling down from overhead. Several couples seemed lost in each other, one couple was ordering drinks and laughing at a joke the waitress had told. The red and orange of the setting sun spread from the horizon, making a delicious backdrop to the small island off the coast.

Bob and Pam sat and watched in silence, comfortable just being with one another. As the band began to play, Bob stood, lifted Pam to her feet, and gathered her into his arms. He guided her to the dance floor.

Bob looked deep within Pam's eyes as they slowed their dance and held each other and simply swayed with the music.

"Pam, I want us to share the rest of our lives together," he said.

Pam's eyes filled with tears and he brushed them gently away with his finger and kissed her eyes-first the left and then the right. She melted into his body.

Bob reached into his jacket pocket and found the ring he had placed there.

Gently brushing her hair away from her ear, he whispered, "My love, will you marry me?"

Pulling herself back from his tight embrace, Pam placed her finger to his lips.

"Oh, yes."

The music played. Their bodies moved as one.

Bob carefully orchestrated the ring onto her finger and drew her close. He smiled and thanked all that was good for her and for the promise of their new life together.

For a while the family groups enjoyed the thrill of the spontaneous muddy vibrations. They were tumbled and tossed until the energy returned to wholeness. Then they breathed, relaxed and laughed. Eventually the next wave of distorted energy would take them into discordant harmonics causing another rush. Returning to their clear state always brought relief. So, the experiment continued swinging from balance to imbalance, calm to panic. The swings soon became difficult, the energy heavier and sluggish. The family members were feeling pain that they had not known before. Finally, one of the twelve family groups was ready to be stabilized.

But doubt had begun to creep among the thirteenth group observing from the deck, cold fingers of fear. What had seemed like an easy task, reaching out to stabilize each group, now created doubts. Will we be strong enough? Will the sticky energy entrap us? What if we get sucked into their chaos?

The family members in the thirteenth group were not certain that they could fulfill their assignment. There was conflict, pleading, reasoning and shattered focus.

Such was the situation within the thirteenth when the first group in the chaos experiment reached out. Ready for the experiment to stop they called to the thirteenth for help.

There was no answer.

They called again. No response came.

Fear escalated. It became harder to breath.

Menacing energy surrounded them.

One by one, the twelve family groups were left uncorrected. Their vibrations slowed, chaos and fear grew. The experiment had gone badly wrong.

They had been abandoned, they were dying. And then more.

Oh god, sticky, clawing tentacles reached out, hooking to their bodies. Attaching, sucking.

Help, please help!

CHAPTER 33

Pam woke suddenly from a restless sleep. She felt clammy. A knot of terror gripped her throat shortening her breath. She inhaled deeply and breathed to force the tightness out into the room.

She looked around her into the dark of the night and psychically called for Shadow.

"Shadow, please have the angels TAG and Transform what is causing this feeling," she trembled. It took several requests before her body relaxed.

Pam lay back onto her pillow, closed her eyes, and searched for the source of this terror. She reviewed her activities of the past week; her clients had made amazing breakthroughs, the children's project was bringing a deep sense of satisfaction, and then there had been the wonderful weekend with Bob.

Suddenly, she knew the problem. It was Bob.

She thought of spending her life with him, and the terror came back. Acknowledging its presence, she rode the fear. Like a wild horse, she felt it rush and pause, lift and settle. Knowing that this emotion had a message to give her, she became the observer, detached and alert.

"Who within me can tell me about this terror?" she asked of herself and then Pam waited.

Slowly her mind stilled and a voice whispered, "I can, but we must be very quiet."

"What name can I call you?" Pam held a conversation with the voice as if she were talking with a child or a client.

"You may call me what you will. My name does not matter. What does matter is that you are in danger. You can bring great harm to others," were the words that came to her mind.

"I do not understand," Pam was startled.

"If you come together with the one you call Bob, they will see your great light and destroy both of you," came the words.

"Who will see?" she asked.

"Those who do not want there to be Light," was the reply.

"And so you bring this terror to warn me?" Pam asked.

"Yes. It is necessary that you be small, be still, do your life in invisible ways. He must do the same. It is not safe to be together," the voice concluded.

Pam listened. Then, she asked questions of this one who brought terror. She listened as if she were conversing with another person until Terror had no more to say.

"I thank you for the warning," Pam spoke solemnly. Then she called to Shadow.

"Shadow, I would like to go back to the time I created this belief."

She relaxed and let herself move to another time and place. With several deep, long breaths she was there.

Pam saw herself. She was in a female body. She was helping to launch a boat. There was a group of people around her. She was looked up to as the leader although everyone there had great value; each had a piece to contribute. Like pieces of a puzzle, together they formed a whole.

It was night. They were fleeing their city. No one was to know, there had to be absolute silence. She saw there were children in the boat. Two of them were hers.

Pam asked to see her husband.

The pain she felt at this request flowed from deep within her soul and ached in the very marrow of her bones. She felt the pain rise to her throat. With all the strength of will she had, this young woman contained the anguish and remained completely silent. There must be no sound.

Pam watched as the boat took them away and knew that this young woman was more than a leader. She carried within herself all the knowledge, the plans, and the grid work for a new civilization.

How could that be? Her question was answered instantly.

She and her husband had been in one of many groups that had tried to change the course that was bringing destruction to their city. He was brilliant, as was she. He knew corrections that could turn the tide. He must stay in the hopes that those who ruled Atlantis would listen to him. The chances were slim, but so many people were in danger of being destroyed that he must try.

They had prepared together. Many groups had considered what would be needed to survive. If the corrections were not made, this group would be in a secure land able to begin again. She was to take this group and their children to safety while he stayed behind.

Pam had never felt such devastating pain nor witnessed such courage. She stayed with the unfolding story until she could stand no more.

"Shadow, what did I miss back then? What is Terror showing me?"

"You did not miss anything. You did that lifetime perfectly. So perfectly and strongly that you anchored the vow of silence, the commitment of loss, the life of the hermit. It became your foundation for all future lifetimes on this planet.

"It is time to recognize that you are no longer the leader moving others through such treacherous days. You no longer pose a threat to the man you love by being in his life.

"The one you call Terror is that part of yourself that did the job you gave her, the job of suffering silently while living life alone. Now it is time to relieve her of that role and give her one appropriate for this life."

Pam breathed herself back to the energy presence of Terror.

"Thank you for being so strong and courageous for me and the others. You have kept me safe and I appreciate your diligence," Pam spoke to Terror.

"However, that part of our life is over and I release you from the job of silence and hermit living. Could I please have all that you took on, the script, costumes, and emotions? I'm going to give that energy bundle back to our angels to be transformed into Love and Light."

Pam saw it done and then said to Terror.

"What job would you like to have in my life as it is now?"

She saw Terror soften and smile.

"First, I want the name of Danielle. And I want to help you work with the babies."

"So be it!" laughed Pam. She mentally watched Terror's energy shift from heavy brown into the lightest of blue and green. Pam breathed this part of herself into her heart area. Another fractured piece had been transformed.

CHAPTER 34

Bob and Pam drove into the neighborhood where Rory and Gerri had found their new home. It was in a quaint, older area of town with unique, well-kept homes. It was their first visit since their friends moved in.

The creamy yellow house stood out against the rich green of the spring grass. The home had two stories on the left and one story on the right, a large, covered front porch that extended from the single story with scrolled gingerbread trim. The yellow of the house was softened with white trim on the corners, the upper pitch of roof, as well as around the many windows.

"Well, I'm anxious to get down to business," said Bob as they parked in the driveway. "Are you going to add what you have learned from your new client?"

"No, I am not ready yet. Still a lot to learn," she replied. "There is enough to weave together with what we brainstormed at the lake. If we can lay a good foundation with various processes, that will be the way to start."

Yellow daffodils and pink and purple hyacinths filled the areas on either side of the curved path leading to the porch. Rory opened the front doors as Bob and Pam walked up the path.

"Come on in," he said stepping aside for them. "I've had ideas for this follow-up meeting flying through my head all morning. I can hardly wait to get started.

"Gerri has the notes from our brainstorming," Rory continued as she came into the room.

"I'm not ready to share the notes until we get to see the ring!" she said, laughing. Pam glowed as she held out her hand.

"Now we all have new beginnings to share. It was about time you made the commitment," she said turning to Bob and all four reached to hold hands.

Gerri understood that Rory was feeling a little anxious and she smiled. Turning to Pam and Bob she asked, "Where would you like to work, in the kitchen around the table or here in the living room?"

"My preference would be the table, at least for a while," said Bob. "That way I can write as we go along."

"Suits me," said Rory. "What about you?" he asked Pam.

"I like that idea," she said.

Gerri smiled her agreement. "Okay, the kitchen it is," she said and moved the group that direction.

"I really love what you have done with the home," confided Pam to Gerri. "It's so cozy."

"We're really lucky to have found it. There are some things we want to do, but all in good time," smiled Gerri. "And I'm glad that at last you have a ring and a date."

They sat down and Gerri put papers on the table in front of each of them.

"Here are copies of the notes I took. I cleaned them up a little," she said. "We really have some good ideas."

Everyone was quiet as the group read over the notes. They quietly muttered sounds of agreement and approval as they read.

Bob laughed. "I like this one," he said. 'Children act out the hidden family stuff...scary for a mom and dad who would rather keep it hidden.' That's so true!"

Everyone joined in his merriment and then grew silent again.

"Have you all finished?" asked Rory as he stepped up as the facilitator.

They nodded.

"I would like to make some suggestions," he continued. "First, I think that it's critical to make a Reality Shift for our goal. We can use the one I initially wrote as a beginning.

"And then second, what about creating a list of ideas we have about children, about pain, etc. It seems that such a list would let us know what we have to clear in ourselves."

There was agreement and each one settled in for a focused work session.

"You know," Bob volunteered, "I think very few people are willing to admit that they play a major role in creating the situations in their life. It's a concept that many would fight you on."

"Well, I did not come up with the concept. It's mentioned in many religions and philosophies as a governing law of human experience. It's closely linked to freedom and free agency. Whether an individual believes it or not, the result is that as you believe, so are you," returned Rory.

"I agree with you. The reason I bring it up is that we will need to face the fact that many people will not take responsibility for their life situations," concluded Bob.

"Wide spread denial of our part in our creations is very real, especially as it relates to the pain our children are experiencing." Pam spoke up.

The others nodded.

"When I was on the streets, I spend time with lots of homeless kids. I heard about moms who chose an abusive partner over their child and children who had been abused by one family member only to be labeled as the trouble-maker and pushed out if they told. There were some kids whose view of the world didn't fit with the family's, and so were seen as bad rather than as offering a unique view. Being addicted to our limited view of life, we push away what we don't understand. We talk about the value of our children, yet we act in ways that say what we truly value is the status quo. So my question is: do we treat our children like we treat the situations in our life?"

"Explain that a little," asked Rory."

"Well, if the situation is comfortable, we see it as a blessing from God," began Pam.

"Right," there were nods and agreement.

"And if the situation is painful, we see it as a curse meant to confuse and punish us. We call the pain bad, disown that we had any part in bringing it to us, and blame external forces, God, boss, partner, etc., for bringing it to us, some external "they" that created the thorn in our side," said Pam.

"Yes, that is often how people think," agreed Gerri.

"We do the same with our children. If we approve of what they do and how they think, we call them blessings. If their behavior, attitudes, or ideas challenge us or run contrary to our view of a good child, we disown and punish them. That is the comparison I see," concluded Pam.

"I see what you mean," Rory said.

"When you think about it in that way, our life situations are the children of our thoughts and emotions. Our children inherit our genetic patterns, our situations inherit our patterns of thought and emotion," reasoned Gerri.

"Yes," continued Pam. "And to blame the external situation and push it away, or to blame our children for what they show us and push them away, misses the point that we also carry the pattern.

"We could see ourselves in our children just as we could see ourselves in our situations. The ugly, that we refuse to see within ourselves, is shown to us clearly by those around us. The ugliest could come to us through the reflection in our children."

"But, what adults do most often is disown or blame the mirror-which could be a life situation or their child. We see it all the time on a social level. Unfortunately, message givers are often killed by society," spoke Rory.

"Good comparison," he continued. "Well, as we know, there is a lot to be done. Let's get back to work." The others agreed.

By the end of two hours, they had organized their thoughts into a practical plan with some action items.

Gerri's notes read:

1. type organizational plans and include purpose, our basic premises and proposed plan of action

2. place ad in local papers for an information meeting.

3. design flyers for the meeting.

"I think that we can be ready for our first public meeting in four weeks," said Rory his eyes showing his excitement. "Let's meet next week to go over what we want to have in place and to set an agenda. Would that work for you two?" he asked Pam and Bob.

They looked at each other. Bob pulled out his calendar and looked over his commitments. "I could get together then. What about going to place the crystals after the meeting? I'll bring them with me."

Rory and the others were in agreement and the meeting ended.

CHAPTER 35

Their lovemaking was slow and gentle, like there was no time, no meaning except that which they wove with their eyes and bodies: hands dancing over skin, lightly stroking, firmly holding, and then letting go to caress.

The passion of the soul directed the play, while the desire of the body rose in waves. Riding the crests, lips kissed breasts and tongue stroked ear. Eyes ever searching the depths until the depths went too deep to follow, hands moving from firm thigh to muscular back and from thin neck to soft abdomen.

Neither Pam nor Bob had wanted a large wedding. They held a private space for their love. They had chosen a grove protected by several stands of beautiful pine trees and aspens. The grasses grew undisturbed and the ferns were tucked everywhere, even hanging from the trees. Several times they had come to bless this spot and to be blessed by the hands of their Mother, the Earth, and call in the wonderful sun.

The day came. It was perfectly arrayed for them: cloudless blue sky, gentle cooling breeze, and summer flowers in full bloom. Bob and Pam had written their own vows of commitment and love. Their hearts were in every word.

With Rory, Gerri, and a few close friends joining to witness, Pam and Bob stood with a minister they had chosen. Pam took Bob's hands, looked into his eyes and spoke,

"My dearest one,

"I come to you with open hands, loving heart, and feet solidly planted. I come to join my life with yours. This is a choice I make joyously and freely, desiring to expand rather than to contract, wishing to lighten rather than to burden. Trusting Love because I recognize Light, trusting you because I recognize me, trusting togetherness because I recognize singleness, I willingly join you in a path of unity and love."

Lifting her hands to his lips, Bob had continued the ceremony.

"My love,

"My vow to you I have learned from life. Life is magnificent, life is noble, life is constant and flowing. We do not seek life, it rushes to greet us. Life is ever present, offering all of its potential with graciousness and love.

"I could do no better than to share my life with you. I do not take lightly your presence in my world, for I honor and love your being.

"In this moment I pledge to you my self and my heart for our life together."

Had it happened as they planned? Their mystical meeting had been so appropriate. And now they could truly begin their life together. This night of love deepened their bond and opened the depths within them closed so long ago. It was happening, here, now!

CHAPTER 36

Invitations to the first public meeting for the children had been sent to friends and acquaintances. Ads had run in several local publications. Gerri had designed flyers and Pam had prepared applications for those who would like to join them as health professionals or as volunteers.

A local paper had picked up on the project as a possible human-interest story and sent a journalist, Kate Reardon, to talk with Rory. As she sat and discussed Rory's background, his desire to help children, and the group's extensive view, she became very interested. She asked if she could come to the meetings and document their progress. Rory was thrilled for the help.

Rory and Gerri were there early to set up the chairs, a white board for the presentations, and to make sure the room was comfortable. When Bob and Pam arrived, Rory took them and Gerri aside. Together they held hands, reaffirmed the intention for this meeting, and asked for guidance and harmony. Kate Reardon came in shortly after they'd finished. Rory introduced her to the other three. Then he and Bob helped set up her recording equipment while Gerri and Pam laid their information on the table that stood at the back of the room, an easy place for people to pick up papers as they entered or left.

It was five minutes to seven before the first guests arrived. Several of their friends came as well as others they had not yet met. Some came alone, others came as couples, and a few came in groups of three or four. They all took flyers and found seats. Pam's CD player provided quiet background music. Those in the room comfortably read the flyers, whispered with their friends, or simply sat waiting for the meeting to begin. Within five minutes there were over thirty people in the room.

Rory took charge and stood to welcome everyone. He introduced himself, Gerri, Bob and Pam. Then he invited everyone to share how they had heard of this meeting and what their interest was in such a group.

One by one some stood and introduced themselves. Latecomers silently took their seats. Gerri made notes to be added to her files.

Rory thanked them for being there and for their concern for the children.

"All of you probably remember the shooting at Glacier Park. It really distressed me. As a counselor, I see people every day who are struggling with their own pain or that of their children's. That incident spoke to me about our insufficiencies in getting to the heart of some problems.

"Pam is a mystic with valuable insights into the laws of the universe that are always at play and areas unseen by the physical eye. We believe that the physical situations of pain will not go away until we come together and look deeper for answers. Until we do that, we can expect to see the pain and violence in our children escalate, and that is not a happy thought."

Rory took a drink of water and continued. "The four of us have made a commitment to do all in our power to bring together conversations aimed at stopping the violence. We believe that the patterns are not just within children, but within each of us, and that patterns of non-health exist beyond individuals in what some would call mass consciousness.

"Our initial statement of intent is on section three of your flyer." Here Rory read their statement.

"I want to share some statistics with you," he continued. "They were compiled by the Children's Defense Fund.

"In a 2002, 3,012 children and teens were killed by gunfire in the United States. That is one child every three hours. Homicide is the third leading cause of death among children 5 to 14 years old, and the second leading cause of death among young people and adults ages 15 to 24.

"More children and teens died from gunfire than from cancer, pneumonia, influenza, asthma, and HIV/AIDS combined in 1998.

" And from the Centers for Disease Control and Prevention, 'The rate of firearm deaths among kids under age 15 is almost 12 times higher in the United States than in 25 other industrialized countries combined.'"

Rory continued, "As a counselor who sees pain and confusion daily, I feel very passionate about finding deeper healing by expanding into new territory. When I sit with a child that I cannot reach or a parent whose depression I cannot touch, my heart aches for answers.

Rory stopped and looked out over the group. He could see the concern in the faces of the audience and that gave him a sense of hope.

"We are looking for others who want to join us in what we feel is a mission, a mission of saving our children and ourselves. The pain of our children will only escalate until there are adequate solutions.

"On the inside pages of your flyers you will find our basic premises and plan.

"I think it's important that you know we are not affiliated with any religious organization, although we each have our own sense of spirituality or Greater Power. We are very concerned adults who are proposing an eclectic, integrated, open approach to this serious problem."

With that he motioned to Pam. "I have asked Pam to talk a bit about our premises and the integrated plan we have in mind."

The audience gave Rory a respectful applause as Pam walked forward.

"I am very glad to see so many of you here tonight," she began. "I want you to know that we are aware that our basic concepts may push the envelope of comfort for many of you. These concepts are a combination of what we have encountered from working with ourselves and with others. We feel that these concepts must be considered in order to change lives as deeply as is needed.

"They are in your flyers, but we want them recorded for the video and so I will go over the concepts upon which our project will be built:

"First, experiences and decisions made before conception and in the womb have an impact on an individual's life and must be considered.

"Second, souls have personal plans for their life. These plans include patterns of dysfunctionality to heal, skills and interests to develop, and inherited family gifts and garbage to sort through and clean up. Awareness of the composition of individual plans will give us insight.

"Third, the human brain is unorganized at birth. It organizes as an infant searches with his eyes, crawls, walks, etc. From birth to age six is a perfect time to do deep healing to prevent the dysfunctional patterns from organizing into the brain. Additionally, by intentionally focusing on life values and speaking the child's worth, a parent can cause brain neurons to form, and to organize to the concepts a family deems valuable. There is a similar process that takes place during the teen years.

"Four, the brains of children who are abused or neglected become disjointed. These children have been labeled kids with broken brains. Physical activity and brain integration is critical for these children even after they become adults.

"Fifth, our inner patterns will show up in our life as external situations. These situations can lead us to the inner disruptions and hence to deeper healing.

"And Rory has pointed out number six. Dysfunctional patterns that are not discovered and changed when they present themselves with a gentle external expression will escalate into situations that are increasingly painful. We will know if the deeper causes are adequately addressed because when they are, the pain will begin to diminish.

"Those are our basic concepts.

"As we begin working with individuals, we will use several methods to evaluate and shine light on our clients and what is problematic. First, an intuitive look; second, quality medical input, third, good psychological information, and fourth, insight from energetic tools that make energy understandable. This protocol of integration will provide greater awareness, like looking at a diamond from its many facets.

"Our proposal is to create an individualized program from the combined evaluations. We believe that the multi-dimensional parts of human life must be addressed if permanent change is to occur, and so our model will consist of five basic parts.

"Let me draw a model on the board." Pam walked to the white board and spoke as she picked up a marker. She drew a spiral that began at the top of the board and extended to the bottom. She then marked it off into four sections. As she turned around she could see that everyone was sitting forward or was in some way showing interest.

"This spiral represents the life force within an individual. It begin in realms that none of us can see with our physical eyes. Most call it God or Greater Power. That energy flow extends downward indicating energy frequencies whose vibrations slow until, at the bottom of this spiral, we have vibrations perceived with our physical senses. "

Pam went on to indicate the four divisions as the physical, mental, emotional and spiritual or etheric bodies that comprise all human beings.

"In addition," she continued, "there is the energy held as group that must be factored in.

"We will include professionals who have effective processes for each energy body. Some of you may be familiar the concept that the physical body is connected and dependent upon the etheric body for cellular guidance and cannot exist without the etheric body. If the etheric field becomes distorted, physical disease soon follows as organ pathology. In my work, I have found this to be true and therefore an integrated approach works most quickly.

"And we plan to provide space to listen. Our children are now being born with clarity about themselves. We will listen to them and create healthier models that will work for them.

"So that is our plan in a nutshell. We intend to positively impact children and the ones who love them. We intend to stop the pain of our children and are looking for those who would like to work with us and expand our model."

Pam stopped, and then asked. "Are there any questions?"

Everyone sat quietly and then one young woman in the back of the room slowly raised her hand. Pam pointed to her and asked her to stand.

"My name is Evelyn. I read about this meeting in the paper last Tuesday and wanted to come. I didn't know if I would be able to sit through it, but I wanted to try. I wanted to be here to speak for my daughter, Stacy. You do not know me, but you will remember her."

Evelyn's voice choked and she breathed several times to gain control of her emotions. The room was silent. Her deep pain radiated and touched everyone.

"I would like everyone to remember her." She almost whispered the words.

Then she stopped and looked down waiting a moment before she looked up into Pam's eyes and continued, "Actually, I wouldn't care if anyone even knew her if I could be home playing with her right now." Tears streamed down Evelyn's face. "But the gun shots at Glacier Park took her away from me, away from us."

The young, blond-haired man by Evelyn's side reached for her hand and bowed his head. She waited and then continued.

"I don't have answers, just a lot of questions, more than I think you could answer tonight. I just wanted to say that we should do whatever it takes, try whatever may even possibly work, and not be afraid of being unpopular. What would it matter if we could save one child or prevent one mother the pain that I carry every day, or my husband's heartache? I want to be with your group doing whatever I can, for Stacy."

Tears overtook her as she sat down. There was not a dry eye in the room as Pam quietly said, "Thank you, Evelyn. Welcome."

Looking around, Pam sensed that the audience was contemplating Evelyn's words. She glanced at Rory who nodded.

"I don't think there's more I could add. Rory, Gerri, Bob, and I will be available after the meeting and would be more than happy to talk with each of you. We have flyers that you can take for friends and applications for those who think they may want to work with us. If you sign the mailing list, you will be notified of our next meeting.

"Again, thank you so much for being here and for caring."

And with that she walked back to her seat and sat down. Her eyes went to Evelyn and she made a mental note to speak with her before she left. Her words reminded her to spend time with the folder for her new client that lay on her desk and whose presence was never far from her mind.

CHAPTER 37

Gerri was busy cleaning the kitchen windows of their home. The sunny day was making the rain residue even more apparent and with fall days coming, Gerri wanted to grab the opportunity that the sun presented. Today was the time to get the sparkle back into the glass. It felt great to be on the other side of finals, with more time to enjoy their home.

Her pregnancy was easy so far. It was mid-October, and with about three months left, she was very excited about the prospect of motherhood. Warm, maternal feelings welled up whenever she thought of the small one, wrapped in a soft blanket. She could almost smell the new baby's tiny body and touch his wee fingers and toes. Imagining the delight she saw in Rory's eyes brought a smile to her face.

She hummed as she polished the glass with last night's newspaper. It was a trick her mother had taught her. "The ink will make the glass shine," she could still hear her mom's voice in her head.

Gerri heard the sound of Rory's car in the driveway and her heart skipped. She was surprised at how much she loved this man.

The back door opened slightly, but there was no Rory.

Gerri was puzzled; she looked at the door and waited.

She saw the door open a bit more. Still Rory did not come through.

Now she was a little anxious. Maybe it hadn't been Rory's car she had heard.

She moved carefully down from the small step stool and started walking slowly toward the back door.

Suddenly, in rushed a tiny orange ball of fur. Gerri gasped and jumped. The ball scooted past her and leapt onto the living room couch. Rory laughed as he walked through the door toward Gerri.

"What's going on?" Gerri stood with her hands on her hips although she was not able to keep a straight face.

Rory scooped her up in his arms and they both laughed. He kissed her on the forehead.

"Well, my dear, I found this lost little tabby and she just seemed to call out your name. Of course, when I tried to send her in to you, she balked."

As they held each other in the middle of the kitchen, the orange tabby scrunched up her tiny body. Her eyes were on the floor where crumpled newspaper lay. She wiggled her body to get a solid footing and with two major leaps pounced in attack on the rumpled "enemy."

Rory laughed, reached down and lifted her up by the nape of her neck. He placed her gently into Gerri's cupped hands.

Gerri cuddled her and touched the kitten's soft fur with her cheek.

The baby cat reached out a cold, wet nose to Gerri and they looked eye to eye.

"Hi, little one," Gerri crooned. "So you wanted to come here to live did you?"

She felt the soft little body.

"You know, you are close to the color of my topaz stones," Gerri spoke as she turned and looked at Rory. "How do you like Topaz for a name?"

"Sounds like a good one to me," replied Rory. "I stopped and picked up some equipment for her at the store. I'll get it from the car."

Rory moved from the kitchen and closed the back door behind him.

Gerri kissed Topaz between her ears and laid her on the lap blanket on the couch.

"You just relax while I finish my windows," she said.

But no sooner had Gerri picked up a newspaper and the spray bottle then Topaz jumped at the crumpled newspaper and bounded back into the living room.

"So, you are a disrupter of systems, are you? Good preparation for a baby, I suppose."

Smiling, Gerri returned to her window project.

CHAPTER 38

The meeting to make more specific plans had been held at Rory and Gerri's home. Those who had signed the list at the first meeting were invited. About eighteen came with others calling to express interest but with conflicts in their calendars.

Pam and Bob stayed after the planning meeting to help Gerri and Rory tidy up. A lot had been accomplished. There were some concerned parents who were ready to use the project's model with their children.

Gerri and Pam stood at the sink washing cups and spoons talking over the evening's events. Their quiet talk and laughter rippled through the conversation that Rory and Bob were having in the living room. The two men looked in the direction of the kitchen and smiled at one another.

"I think that it would be better if we went to place the crystals this Saturday. What do you think?" Bob asking.

"I don't have any conflicts. I'd like to get an early start, maybe about seven. Would that work for you?" Rory asked.

"Sure, I'll make it work. It seemed right to get thirteen crystals. I don't know where they are to be placed, but I'll get an area map and ask for some insight before Saturday." Bob paused and then said, "The meeting sure went well."

"I guess it's time for us to walk our talk and see where it leads. Let's see, we have Arnold Purkes who is a naturopathic physician. He seemed very excited to be on board. I was glad to see Kirk Jullian. His physical challenge course will be great in working with the kids," Bob contributed.

"Yes," said Rory. "I've worked with Kirk and his team before and have been very impressed with them."

"Now, what was the name of the woman who has been trained in numerology? She spoke quite softly and I missed it." Bob asked.

Rory picked up the sheet where everyone had signed his or her name and address.

Bob ran his finger down the sheet. "Here she is, Janeen Hopkins. I thought I'd have a session with her to see what I think of her work. She took an application, so she'll have some references."

"I thought I'd try the astrologist, Jack." Rory looked down the sheet. "Here he is, Jack Cooper. He seemed very committed to what we are proposing. I think that some first-hand experience with each other will build our collective energy, compatibility, and level of professionalism."

"I agree. I want to walk carefully and slowly. We'll ask Gerri and Pam to design some consent and release forms for the parents. There is a nutritional consultant I want on the team, Karen Hoopes. She has done some amazing work on the correlation between nutrition, addiction, depression and weight. It is exciting to see that the Brownes are hopeful for their daughter and excited for us to work with them."

"Yes," agreed Bob. "And I was glad that Evelyn showed up. She is really quite emphatic that she will do whatever we need. She really wants to make this work. Her husband had some very good questions and suggestions."

"She asked if I would see her as part of her healing program. I'm glad she's paying attention to her pain," volunteered Rory.

"It looks like we have a good group of professionals who want to be a part of this project. As soon as we get their applications and references and do some background checks, we'll see whom to invite. Then we can get together for specific planning and team building. I think we can file our nonprofit papers now and get that process started.

"Also, we probably ought to have a basic organizational chart and plan for clients before we have our next meeting. That way, we will have something concrete to show how the project can be run and everyone can give feedback," Bob said. "Another thing to consider is money. Are we going to write for grants, do some fundraising, or volunteer our time for a while?"

Pam and Gerri finished washing and drying the cups, cleaned up the kitchen, and came into the living room. Rory shifted his attention away from Bob's question when the women came in and it remained unanswered.

Gerry yawned and Rory drew her close to him.

"Thanks for all that you each did to get ready for this meeting," Rory spoke. "We certainly had a great group tonight."

The others smiled and nodded in agreement.

CHAPTER 39

Jim and Linda Browne sat with Pam in her conference room. They had been at both project meetings, looking for answers to their daughter Sara's pain.

Sara was just nine years old and in the third grade. They had recently moved in with Linda's mother while their new home was being built. Jim was working to build a new business and was not home much, and so the parenting fell largely to Linda. Sara had become very clingy, demanding a lot of attention from her mom. They understood that her behavior might have to do with the hours that Jim was away, but she was not doing well in school, either. Sara was easily distracted and having a difficult time with some of her class assignments. This had been going on for quite some time, so Linda had requested that Sara's school counselor do an evaluation. The counselor's opinion was that Sara was suffering from depression and suggested they find a doctor who would give her medication.

They wanted to look for other options. When they saw the flyers for the first public meeting they had come hoping to get some insight. They had liked what they heard, came to the meeting at Rory and Gerri's home, and had taken Pam's business card. Within three days, Linda had called and made an appointment with Pam.

At their first session, Pam sat, listened, and asked a lot of questions. Sara was not a violent child, but clearly she was feeling something that needed to be addressed. After their discussion, Pam recommended a plan.

It included several steps. Sara would have a TAG energy session to evaluate and balance her energy fields. Whatever soul issues had been activated could be cleared. Also, Pam would do an etheric and Indigo child evaluation with Sara to discover what gifts and deep patterns the child had brought in for this lifetime. Then they would ask Jack Cooper to draw up Sara's astrology chart to see what her planetary energy picture could tell, have Karen evaluate diet and nutrition and then they would have sessions with Dr. Allen Purkes and Rory.

Jim and Linda had signed release forms with the understanding that each professional's commitment was to do no harm. It was also understood that the information shared among the professionals was for the purpose of empowering the parents with more options, and that the final decision as to what would best serve their child was to be made by the parents. The parents were asked to give truthful feedback. There would be a pre-evaluation, a period of time agreed upon with a suggested program, and written feedback. It was clear that they could choose to leave the project at any time.

Linda and Jim had been thrilled by the plan. Now they were back in Pam's office to discuss what changes they may have noticed with Sara and to ask more questions.

"It was rather late by the time we got home after your work with Sara," Linda said. "Usually she rummages through the refrigerator, whines about her schoolwork, begs to sleep in our room, and reluctantly goes to bed.

"Well, she didn't whine at all. In fact she had only a drink of juice, then came into our room and picked up her blanket and pillow. I was surprised so I asked her what she needed." Linda was smiling as she told the story.

"She stopped and looked at me very thoughtfully. Then she said, 'Mom, I'm almost ten years old. I think I should be sleeping in my own room.' Then as she was leaving, she stopped, turned around like she had just had a new thought. 'And besides,' she said, 'I'm not scared any more.'

Jim added his observations. "For the past week she has been more confident. Another thing, she is getting her homework done with much less hassle."

"Well," interjected Pam, "remember that old pattern she was carrying from a lifetime when her mom had died when she was ten years old. TAG provides command and space for the fear patterns to be released and it sounds like it has been."

CHAPTER

Pam had decided to look up Nancy who she had met at the Center. Now Nancy worked at the neo-natal unit in a local hospital. She didn't know why the thought had come to her, but she had made the call.

She walked through the labyrinth of halls wondering what she would say. Her inner voice was urging her on, a voice she had never regretted following.

Pam saw the door to the neonatal unit ahead of her. She pushed on the double doors and walked toward the nurse's station. As she got closer, Pam noticed Nancy's familiar face. Pam slowed as she observed her moving from behind the station. As Nancy moved past the counter she lifted her head and their eyes met.

Nancy smiled. "Hi, Pam. This is good timing. I'm just about ready for my dinner break. We can go to the cafeteria and talk," invited Nancy.

"I'd love that," replied Pam. "It's good to see you again."

The walk through the halls was easier with Nancy leading the way and by the time they were in the cafeteria, the two women had caught up on some events of their lives that had transpired since the Center.

Nancy spoke, "I'm so glad you called. I've thought about you and wondered what you were up to, wondered if you were still working with stones and spirit." She laughed at the thought, walked over to the hospital's cafeteria line, and picked up a brown plastic tray.

Pam followed her and placing her tray on the metal counter answered, "I sure am! Still doing stones and far out work. You know I've been working with lots of adults and most recently have been working with babies and children. The other day I just felt I needed to come see you."

They each absently picked up dishes of food from the selections under the clear canopy.

"Actually, I've thought about you, but not taken the time to call. Caught up in my own world I guess." Nancy laughed. "So what has been going on for you?"

"Well, after working with my own pain and finding some answers, I began sharing my work with others and it seemed to help them. So I have continued to learn more ways to help people move out of their inner injuries." Pam ended.

"How ironic," Nancy volunteered. She moved her tray to the cashier's station and paid. Going to the beverage counter for a hot cup of coffee, she heard Pam respond.

"Why is that?"

"Well, because I am searching for answers."

Nancy and Pam carried their trays to an empty booth in a very empty cafeteria. They slid along the bench and Nancy continued, "The work in the unit is so vital and yet it can really take its toll on the professionals as well as the patients and families. I have been wondering if I made a wise choice when I went into this field. Is this really where I belong, and can I keep up with what is required?" Nancy was on the edge of tears.

Pam sat and listened. As she did, some of her experiences flashed in her mind. When Nancy finished, Pam ventured, "I have a thought. Would you like to hear it?"

Nancy cleared her throat as Pam took a bite of her blueberry muffin.

"I'm looking for answers, remember. Sure I would."

Pam swallowed the bite of muffin and sipped her tea. "Well, as I look at life, I see purpose in all of our experiences. When we are knee-deep in our mess, so to speak, it's hard to remember there's value in our pain."

Then as Nancy ate her sandwich and chips, Pam shared her idea about reminding children of their value from the time they are born.

Pam ate more of her muffin as she let Nancy sit with the possibility that such little ones are very aware. Then she continued, "Maybe one of the reasons you're here in this unit with those struggling for life is that you need to speak truth to these babies.

"They need to remember that this experience has a purpose; they need to remember that angels are there with them; and they need to know that you know that they know and they are not alone. Maybe you are here because they need to know that you know this about them."

Nancy ate her meal silently as she contemplated what Pam was saying to her.

Then Pam looked at her over the edge of her coffee cup. "You remember at the Center how I worked with Reality Shifts to anchor new patterns?" asked Pam.

Nancy nodded. "Now that you mention it, I do remember."

"Here's a possible Reality Shift you could use, 'I give thanks that by speaking love and truth to the babies in my care their hearts are touched and their pain lifted. I relax and respond to each. I am inspiring amazing lives.' "

"Now, that's exciting to think about," whispered Nancy. She leaned back on the seat and took a deep breath. Then she reached for Pam's hands. "I'm glad you called. I'm going to give it a try when I go back on shift. Let's write the words down."

And as Pam dictated, Nancy wrote.

Nancy stood. "I have to get back to the floor."

The two lifted their trays and took them to the clearing station. Then they walked briskly from the cafeteria. At the elevators Nancy stopped and took Pam's hand.

"Thanks so much for being who you are. I'll let you know how this goes."

"I'd really appreciate that," Pam responded and then pulled Nancy close for a warm hug. "In fact, let me put my e-mail address by the Reality Shift and you can just e-mail me when you have feedback."

"Great. I'll do that," promised Nancy.

The elevator opened. The two smiled, hands raised in good-by, and Pam strode down the hall to the front door with a light heart.

CHAPTER 41

Several weeks had passed since Pam had visited with Nancy. Then an e-mail came as Nancy had promised. It read:

"Dear Pam:

"Thank you so much for the insight you gave me in the hospital. Sorry I haven't written sooner but you know time.

"I have been telling the babies, 'Little one, I know that what you're going through is not easy.' I cradle their little heads and tiny bodies as I telepathically talk with them.

"But you are going somewhere with all this. There is a direction. You do have a task. You also have everything you need in order to accomplish this task. Every situation brings you something that you can use toward the vision you hold. In case you forget that you do know these things, there are always angels here with you, especially in this place. They will be with you constantly through your life! You can turn to them whenever things seem hard, whenever you forget why you are here, or whenever you do not understand why you have to go through this unpleasant stuff.'

"The first few times I tried this was with "growing preemies," infants who are past those early critical stages of using high-tech to continue their life. These little ones are stable in isolates, but they are not yet able to perform functions like feeding and controlling their own body temperature. They spend much of their time sleeping in an artificial womb.

"One busy night I was behind schedule. One baby's feeding was half an hour late. I was tense. This particular infant was getting phototherapy, a treatment for newborn jaundice. The treatment required that she lay naked in her small glass box with a mask over her eyes while bright lights flooded her small square world.

"She was hungry, wet, and screaming. She flailed her long skinny limbs about, turning her head such that the mask slipped sideways. Now the mask was no longer covering her eyes, but was over her nose instead. She was mad!

"I reached hastily in through the portholes, changed her wet diaper, turned off the bright light, and removed her mask. Suddenly, I saw her and remembered that this was a little human being in distress. This is the moment I thought of you.

"I placed one hand atop her head and tenderly covered the front of her three-pound torso with my other hand. I ceased to approach her with rote, purposeful movements of "gotta change your diaper, now..." and shifted into being present. I relaxed my own shoulders, let out my breath, and emptied my awareness of everything else. I began to speak softly to her from the silence of my mind as well as with my touch. With soft gentleness my skin met hers. It was a respectful, deliberate meeting of energy forms: hers and mine.

"I know you're hungry. The milk that your momma pumped for you is warming. I know that you came here expecting something very different; soft voices, loving snuggles in dim-lit rooms, familiar smells, and someone who would come whenever you called. Instead you find empty air, bare skin, blindfolds, and hot lights! I know you must feel very confused with all you've found here. But it won't always be like this. Already, you have come so far.

"Once you go home, where everyone is eagerly waiting for you, all this will fade. You are where you're supposed to be, doing the work you came here for.

"I don't know exactly what it is, but you do. And your angels have been with you every step of the way. They are watching over you and helping you. Though you may think you have forgotten all that you knew before your arrival on this planet, there is a place inside of you that does remember.

"When it gets too hard for you, all you have to do is turn to your angels and say help! They will be your memory and your strength. All you have to do is ask."

"Each time I did this, I would notice the infants becoming still, quiet and attentive. There was a resonance between us, a release of their tense muscles, as if they truly "got it"! I noticed that if my attention wandered, their response wavered as well. Crying or frenetic activity would resume.

"One night I was assigned to a 29-week preemie who weighed 1 pound. He was on a ventilator and had umbilical catheters with numerous IV lines running into them. Multiple electrodes, to monitor body functions, were attached wherever his fragile skin had an available spot. His blood pressure had been chaotic all day, darting from too high, to too low. His heart murmur was loud. It's a common problem that happens when fetal circulation resumes after birth, causing some unoxygenated blood to be pumped back out by the heart.

"I was quite busy giving medicine, changing IVs, taking vital signs, and measuring fluids. And all the while he was becoming extremely agitated. Morphine sulfate had been ordered as a sedative to calm him if necessary. I decided to take a moment to "talk and touch" my tiny patient before resorting to the use of morphine. Since I felt rather pressured myself, I began by closing my eyes. I planted my feet firmly to connect myself to Mother Earth, and then without to the web of interconnectedness that encircles all of us.

"I wrapped one hand around his miniature head and placed my other hand over his tiny trunk. I asked his angels to do some calming work. And then we had a great little session with one another!

"Before I continued, I glanced about the unit to make sure others were busy. My back was turned to the rest of the nursery so no one would notice me standing here doing this weird thing! Then, I invited him to hear that I knew of his loneliness, frustration, and outrage. I silently explained, "We're trying to simulate your mother's womb since you left it way too soon. I realize this is a far cry from your expectations of loving arms, gentle eyes, a warm breast. Instead you have encountered noises, tubes, and smells, textures and insults.

"But you are not here by accident. There is meaning for you even in this very experience. In fact, you even know what it is, why this is happening, and how to work with it so it serves you and your family!"

"I told him about his angels, how he was not alone, how he could ask for their help. He calmed down. I calmed down. It felt sort of like the way breastfeeding endorphins help moms as much as babies!

"Shortly after I stopped, having returned to my worktable to continue my charting, I looked up at the monitor and was stunned! For the first time in over 24 hours, without any change in medications or treatment, his blood pressure had returned to normal and it stayed that way for hours! I could no longer hear his heart murmur. He rested peacefully for quite some time.

"All the special IV drips we'd given him had failed to do anything for his blood pressure or to calm him. I was quite impressed. If this is coincidence, it is a pretty amazing one!

"Full-term infants are also admitted to the neo natal intensive care unit. Infections are a common reason for this and, unfortunately, the antibiotics they need wreak havoc on their sensitive digestive systems. Diarrhea causes sore bottoms and cramping.

"One huge 10-pound boy was inconsolable. I tried to feed him but he continued to scream and squirm in my arms. So I put the bottle down and began to rock him. I pulled him close to me, encircling him with one arm so that my hand wrapped about his middle. I cradled his head with my other hand and hummed a bit as we rocked.

"Then I talked to him, "It's okay to cry. I know it hurts but it won't always be this way. Don't judge this earth by this harsh beginning. In fact, this is all part of the design in your plan. There is meaning in everything and you can find it. Your parents really love you. They want to take you home so badly! Maybe it helps just a little to know you are not limited to this pain or this body. And you're not alone, not for even a moment. You have helpers and they can ease your distress for you. Let's ask them right now for help and you can remember to do this yourself any time you need to."

"As he softened in my arms, I genuinely wondered, "Who is healing whom, here?" Arms full of warm baby, I felt "the soothing-ness" pass between us. As his frantic, angry cry subsided, the hurting, needy child in me drew upon the solace and strength as well!

"While I have included this work of the soul, I have been reminded that each baby is a unique being whose path has crossed mine at just this moment. Our energies connect and I seek to meet with him or her beneath all the physical stuff. We are no longer separate. This is a truth that is already quite real for newborns and their grief seems to be that they find no adults who reflect this truth. As we meet, the healing simply IS. I have found that it effortlessly exists in such space and enfolds us both.

"When a new soul arrives in this strange place called Earth, she is surrounded by distracted adults going about their business, impervious to the wide-open conscious awareness in which our babies still operate. It must be chilling and disorienting.

"Imagine instead, that adults pierce through the automatic routine and separation that we have come to accept as normal and say to the infant, "I am here. I see you. I can feel you. I can touch you. I am with you." When this is conveyed by heart-mind (whether silent or spoken aloud), an actual bridge is formed.

"Thank you, my friend. I am loving my work!

"Nancy"

Pam printed out the message. She closed her eyes and could sense her inner Danielle laughing with joy.

CHAPTER 42

How many times this picture has been repeated, thought Pam. It was ages old and yet wonderfully new.

Gerri lay cradling her tiny new babe in her arms. Rory perched on the side of the bed, his arm around his wife's shoulders. The son's tiny fingers encircled his dad's large index finger.

At times such as these, words were unnecessary. Love and delight have their own silent language. This gift of a new life had taken Rory and Gerri into a world where nothing else seemed to exist. Joy and reverence permeated the space.

Pam looked into Bob's face. He was smiling. She snuggled closer and circled her arm tighter around his waist. He looked down at her and kissed the top of her head.

Pam ached to hold little Daniel, but she could see that Gerri and Rory were in a world apart. To break the spell cast by his presence would not be appropriate.

She looked up at Bob and whispered, "I think we ought to go home and let them be alone."

Bob nodded.

"Gerri and Rory, thank you for the honor and glorious gift of walking Danny's birth with you. What a miracle," Pam said.

"It's been a long night, so we're going to go on home now, but we'll see you tomorrow," Bob added.

Pam and Bob moved toward the bed and Pam gently stroked Daniel's soft, tiny fingers.

"Remember, there are angels here for you little Daniel," she whispered.

"Thank you so much for your love and help," said Gerri. "It was such a blessing to us."

Pam stroked Gerri's hair. "I love you, my sister, my friend," she said.

Rory moved, beginning to stand.

"No, you stay right there," Bob spoke as he held his hand on Rory's shoulder. "Enjoy your family. We'll be back tomorrow."

Bob and Pam moved out of the room holding hands as they found their way out of the hospital.

Six Klicons from Home

Generation after generation after generation the fall continued, the family's vibrations slowed, and their fear escalated. No one was coming to rescue them. Many ideas had been tried. The best they could hope for was to survive. Now, a new Council had been called.

The new Galactic Council was composed of members representing each family group. The Council was discussing how to deal with the Outsider's monitoring and the continuing experiment's sporadic flips into chaos. It was Jerra's turn to speak.

"It is clear that nothing productive will come out of our discussions when fear and chaos are present. It is equally clear that we each have learned to identify when chaos is getting ready to slip in."

There was nodded agreement.

"So," he continued, "I propose that we agree that discussions will occur only when every Council member is stable, in wholeness. When anyone senses the fear moving in, that member is to call a halt to discussions and we all stop."

Dana expanded, "What I hear is that we must each be in a state of balance or wholeness during discussions."

"That's right," Jerra responded.

"And when one individual senses a slipping out of balance, that member is to stop the discussions," added Tier.

"Yes, that is what I propose," said Jerra.

"That will handle our problem of sporadic fear and chaos," Tuma said. "What about the monitoring of the parasitics? We can't let them know we are planning again."

"Absolutely," spoke Sela. "What if we secret the notes whenever we adjourn no matter what the reason. The plans themselves will always be hidden."

"Keeping our energy fields distasteful to the Outsiders would discourage their monitoring," suggested Myra. "We have learned that they gather around fear, and rush to addictive highs. So it will be up to each of us to

discipline our selves to act as if we are stupefied, with nothing going on," suggested Myra.

And so the Council met and planned. It was painstaking, methodical and slow. And even as they planned, the family fell further into greater discord and danger. They were now seven klicons away from their Divine Home.

Eventually the plan was complete. The next world would make it possible for energy to harden in order to perceive it's source; wholeness, fear or parasitic evil. Individual choice to discern and act was necessary as to quickly identify and remove the Outsiders. And having two body suits; one with the parasitic contract energy and one without contracts to command their removal would finally free the family of invading parasites.

Earth came into being with high hopes.

CHAPTER 43

Pam and Bob quickly parked their car in the hospital parking lot and rushed to the front double doors. The hospital was brightly lit, people coming and going despite the late hour. Their long weekend out of town had been cut short with one frantic phone message, "Come as soon as you can. We need you!"

"Did Rory say where they took Danny?" asked Pam.

"Yes," replied Bob. "Their message said Danny had been taken to the New Haven Children's Hospital. He said that they knew we were out of town, but would we come as quickly as we could. He said they are in the intensive care unit. The call came in earlier today. Maybe he's better by now," Bob hoped out loud.

Pam heard him but didn't answer. Danny was only three weeks old. What could have happened? She continued to call her friends in Spirit and ask for blessings of health and strength for Danny, Rory, and Gerri.

Gerri's mom and dad, appearing very tired and drawn, came around the corner under the sign that pointed the way to the intensive care unit.

Pam called their names and they looked up. Pam reached out to hold Gerri's mom. Tears rolled silently down their faces.

Bob and Gerri's dad shook hands.

"How is he doing?" asked Bob.

"Not very good. He's a strong little guy, but this is a big one," answered Gerri's dad.

"I can't believe this is happening," sobbed Gerri's mom. "It's unreal. We're all so exhausted. We've been here all day. Just need to get some rest. I don't know how the kids are holding up. It's hard to leave but we can't help here," she concluded.

Pam asked, "What happened? We just called our voice mail and there was Rory's message."

"No one knows for sure. The baby was fine, a little fussy last night, but they thought he was just over tired.

"This morning they heard strange, loud, gurgling sounds coming from the nursery. When Gerri checked, Danny's body was jerking and he had a high fever. By the time the paramedics got there, he'd slipped into a coma." Gerri's mom struggled with tears in her voice.

"The hospital has taken a lot of tests, but no one has any answers," finished Gerri's dad.

Pam gave Gerri's mom another hug and squeezed Gerri's dad's hand.

"You two go on home. We'll look after Gerri and Rory and Danny," she said.

"Thanks," Gerri's dad said as he took his wife's hand and the two continued down the hall.

Pam looked up into Bob's eyes. "This is serious."

He shook his head and they turned the corner that led down the hall to the IC unit. A large sign on the door read: "Family Only. Check in at the nurse's station."

Pam looked at Bob.

"Don't worry honey. I'll get us through."

They opened the doors and walked up to the nurse's station.

"We're here for Danny," began Bob.

The nurse on duty looked up.

"Oh, you must be Gerri's sister and brother-in-law. Come, I'll show you to the room."

Pam looked at Bob in surprise. He smiled and squeezed her hand. The nurse quietly opened the door to room 216 and stepped aside to let them in.

Gerri looked up. Seeing Pam and Bob, she began to cry. Pam held Gerri. Bob went over to the tiny crib in which Daniel lay with wires and tubes coming from his tiny body.

Rory was holding his son's tiny hand. The pain in his eyes was so great that he couldn't look up.

Bob gently touched Rory's shoulder, knowing that Rory had put up an intense energy shield to numb his feelings. It was the only way he could be strong for his wife and son. Instinctively, Bob knew that if he were to disrupt that shield, Rory would be lost in the whirling pain. Their eyes met and they both knew that keeping distance was the support Rory needed right now.

Gerri sobbed into Pam's shoulder.

"Shall we go into the waiting room?" asked Pam. Gerri nodded and the two sister friends left Danny with his dad and Bob.

In the small waiting room, Gerri cried as she told Pam the story.

It was as her mother had said. There were no answers. Danny was hooked-up to machines to monitor his body's functions, machines to give him oxygen, machines to give him food, and other machines to give him medications. That he was so young gave them hope.

The nurses and aide were extremely good with him, and he had the best medical doctor in the city. All they could do was wait and watch what his body would do. The doctors had mentioned possible brain damage, no one knew if he had been deprived of oxygen or if there were tumors. It was all extremely frightening. All Gerri wanted was for her son to wake up and smile. She wished that this bad dream would go away so they could bundle him up and go back home.

Gerri's sobs lessened as she curled onto the small sofa, Pam's arms around her. Pam pulled a blanket over her friend and let her rest. Mentally, Pam focused on her guides and called them into the room.

"Shadow, is there a healing team in place with Danny?" she asked as she shifted her inner focus to hear his voice.

"Yes, love, there is," came the reply. "And there is purpose for Daniel, part of the reason is that you are in his life."

Pam was dumbfounded. "Am I the cause of this?"

"No, little one," Shadow answered. "But remember that I told you that you knew the basics and that before long you would bring them together into a bigger picture?"

"I remember," Pam whispered.

"Well, on this planet it was for the males to hold the crown and heart space for nurturing, to flow the sacred and move it out into the world through the power of their heart. Their strength is founded on unconditional love for those with whom their heart resonates. And, it is you, the female, who are to design space, create the environment."

"I don't understand," questioned Pam.

"Well, there is a lot that you will have to take on trust tonight. What is important for you to know is that Daniel needs you to speak with authority. He needs to be able to go through this drama without interference.

"The womb represents space for gestation, birthing and creative renewal. This situation is Daniel's birth out of his old limits. Old disrupted energy would make him vulnerable to negative forces and their attachment would alter the outcome. You are here to hold secure boundaries and demand that his space remain clear and balanced. Then the limits from his past can be addressed and transformed."

"I know that I can trust you, Shadow. I can see the wisdom of that kind of request." Then Pam said firmly, "I want to hear more when things are settled. Now, I just want what is best for my friends."

Then Pam bowed her head and spoke softly, "I command and declare that Daniel is surrounded by Guardians of Light who prevent anything false or distorted from coming into his space. I declare his room Sacred ground. Shadow, I ask that frequencies stabilize his energy centers and that they be filled with the frequencies that are best for his health. Activate the TAG Matrix for Transformation." Pam paused. Then she requested, "Let me know when that is done."

She held Gerri in her arms as she mentally held the focus for Danny's energy fields and boundaries for his space.

"It is done," she heard quietly within her mind.

Psychically, Pam saw herself next to Danny's bed. She called in his higher consciousness and asked for guidance. She re-affirmed that Danny's room be held as Sacred space for frequencies of light, love, and Spiritual healers. In her inner vision she laid her hands on Danny's head and activated the processes of the TAG Matrix.

Mentally she held the focus for the removal of all trauma energy, and disruptive emotions, and asked for continuous healing. She watched with her inner sight as the healers and angels lovingly worked with Danny.

"All is done for now, little one. We will be with him," she heard Shadow say. "Do not worry, there is purpose in this."

So saying, Shadow's presence faded.

There in the waiting room with Gerri, Pam remembered Nancy's experience in the neonatal unit and she made a mental note to share Nancy's experiences with Rory and Gerri.

CHAPTER

Pam sat by the side of Daniel's hospital bed. Gerri and Rory had gone home for some much needed rest. She had talked with Gerri and Rory about Nancy's work with the babies. It seemed to help a bit. Of course, what Rory and Gerri really wanted was for all of this to be over.

The four friends had worked out a plan so that someone could be with Daniel every minute until he was back in his own crib. Today it was Pam's turn to watch and hold command for the health for this tiny one. Gerri was home sleeping and would be back in ICU to spend the night.

Many questions floated through Pam's mind. Questions that needed answering. The biggest one was, "Why?"

Why had this happened to Daniel after all that they had done? And what was it that Shadow meant that she was part of this situation? She had been asking for answers. Now she hoped answers would be given, here with Daniel.

Pam reached for his tiny hand.

"Oh, my little friend. How I wanted to spare you from situations such as this. What did I miss?" She gently kissed the soft, relaxed fingers she held.

"Oh, but you are the one who made this possible!"

Pam sat up straight and looked around. Who had spoken? The voice was clear and deep and strong. But no one was in the room.

"Who is here?" she asked mentally. The question was answered with a clear, strong thought.

"I am the one you call Daniel, and I thank you for this gift."

"The gift of coma, the gift of sorrow? You would call these gifts?" responded Pam.

"Oh yes, my dear one. The soul deepening and forgiveness I desire is possible only in this way. My inner changes are vastly more important than that pain is avoided or even that my physical life continues. With your presence and abilities, I can achieve soul change that can free me from lifetimes of angry, hate-filled experiences and from the control of external forces."

"Daniel, I trust that you know the bigger plan." Pam began. "What boggles my mind is that in all of my work with your mom and dad, I did not see the possibility of this event. Can we start with that? Can you explain to me why?"

"Of course. Your work makes a path for higher evolution possible. My accident, as they call it, was necessary for my evolution. Therefore, the plans for it were hidden from you. It had to happen for my greater expansion to occur. The pattern for this event had to be left.

"But, because of all that you and my parents did, many, many of the old, unresolved patterns of anger, lack, and mistrust were transformed and released before I was born. Many that would have muddied my life, adversely affected others, or caused greater garbage energy for the planet were transmuted. It is a great work you are doing, especially for babies," he concluded.

"Tell me a little more about my work as a gift to you if you still had this horrendous experience to walk through," puzzled Pam.

"First, you must know my background. I have been one who used power to entrap others. I took what I wanted with no regard. I consciously planned and did evil things. I'm sorry to say this, but I spent many lifetimes using power for dark purposes.

"When you, Bob, Gerri, and Rory first came to the planet to help humankind step back into their Divine right of sovereignty, you stood for all that I wanted suppressed. I was determined that you not succeed!"

Pam gasped. Instantly she knew this soul's identity.

"You were Lucas, the leader of the Earth Council and the ancestor of Dean, the one who raped Gerri!"

"Yes." There was sadness in his voice.

"Now you sense a portion of the wrongs I have done. It took many lifetimes before the consequences of my devastating actions began to come back to haunt me.

"It seems as though I have spent eons awakening. It has taken untold pain, much evaluating and planning between incarnations, and hard work to get to where I am now. I have learned that even a small kernel of evil within the human psyche will cause massive pain and harm.

"When our family called forth chaos vibrations in worlds well before Earth, we didn't know that the unlimited faces of chaos would take us so far from our Divine nature. I am ready to release all of my energies of distortion and evil. It is in a physical body that we can complete our healing.

"Gerri and Rory do not remember the promises we made to one another before our births into this lifetime. I promised Gerri that I would help deepen her sense of her divinity and power. To Rory, I committed to bring inner peace. His blame of himself for the rape I inflicted upon Gerri in their first lifetime eons ago still blocks his inner peace. That guilt drives his life.

"Their promise to me was to allow me to bring my commitment to love into the physical realm. This experience will finally transmute the negative energy I created in so many lifetimes. So you see there is glorious purpose for what is called an accident.

"But how do I fit," asked Pam.

"I needed a space secured from Outside societies who had preyed upon my vulnerability, my fears and my greed. You have authority, to hold a clear command and listen to your inner guidance. There is another gift you bring, your mission as a female to remove evil. You can set boundaries, clear energy and secure my space as I release the old trappings."

There was silence.

Pam sat back to think. She remembered the client who had made her aware of the parasitic invaders.

"Do you mean that you have felt the influence of the parasitics who have kept us trapped?"

"Those are the ones I mean."

"Then my leadership of the Sihedaa mission is part of your life also. Is there a clear plan for this?" she asked.

"Quite clear as an end result. A little flexibility as to how it will unfold. I know that I need your knowledge and experience to accomplish my goal. What would you suggest?"

Pam picked up Daniel's tiny hand and gently stroked it. The medical monitoring systems clicked and hummed. She let her focus shift to her Spiritual team. The information from Daniel would not be shocking if she were in her office with a client, and so why should it surprise her here?

Pam remembered Gerri's experience after being raped by Dean three years ago. There was such a massive amount of healing she was able to do around the greater wound from the abusive rape by Driva those lifetimes ago. Pam could see, once again, how everything was part of a bigger picture.

Pam called to her guide, Shadow and listened.

"Well, here is your opportunity to be the clear professional beyond the caring, empathetic friend. Treat this as you would with any one else who is in a crisis situation," reminded Shadow.

Pam reaffirmed the space and boundaries for protection and safety. She took four stones from her pocket, blessed them, and placed them in the four corners of Daniel's hospital room.

"I again claim this room as Sacred space filled with Universal Light. In this room, Daniel's soul intent must be honored."

She reaffirmed the TAG Matrix of transformation around Daniel's tiny body and asked for angels to be placed to maintain the grid of wholeness and the Divine decree of universal laws. She also commanded that there be no invasion of distorted energies or outsiders allowed into this vulnerable situation. Then, Pam evaluated the energy centers and circuitry within Danny's body. The DNA was fully activated with the basic 12-strands, the communication center at the base of Danny's skull was clear and his energy system flowed according to the Divine pattern.

"Keep looking," she heard Shadow say. "There is something for you to find."

Pam scanned Danny's body. She felt the energy, the vibrations, the heat, and the colors. Deeper and deeper she probed. Energy within energy. Moving from the area around his feet, slowly, patiently up his legs she moved her focus.

And then she found them! Hidden in vibrational regions far below physical frequencies at his crotch. Two dark, sticky chips. They were wired into the testicles and had a thin wires leading away from the body. What was it?

"Remove it and we will take it back to its place of origin," Shadow was telling her. "You are seeing energy forms that represent the contracts made to the Outside societies. We will talk more about them later."

Pam held her focus on the chips. Commanding an end to the contracts made in other regions, she stood firm. Evil and threatening forms were arrayed around the room trying to stop her.

"What?" she reached out to ask Shadow.

"Simply hold space, you have the right and they no longer do." came the response.

She manipulated the energy chips, neutralizing and then disconnecting them. Instantly, she was free of the stickiness and the threatening forms dissolved.

Danny heaved a sigh from deep within his chest. A slight smile, turn of his head and then peace.

Next Pam called the souls of Daniel, Gerri, and Rory into the room.

As they appeared to her, Pam mentally explained to Gerri and Rory the role that Daniel had played in their lives in that long ago time. Even in this mental space, they struggled with that thought. The love they felt for Daniel, as their precious son, was so clear and present. The residue of anger they felt toward the one they had known as Driva, rose from a place they had not known still existed. Driva, the one whose evil had left patterns for his genetic family line. He was the soul embodied as their son?

Pam noticed their struggle and asked that the TAG Matrix be placed around each of them. The Matrix lightened the anger and allowed space for Gerri and Rory to detach from the long ago experience with Driva. The energy that radiated from this soul as their son, Daniel, was a testament to the awareness he had achieved, his work to heal, and his commitment to walk with light and love.

Gerri turned to Pam.

"What is asked of us in relationship to the lifetime with Lucas?"

Pam listened to Shadow.

"He is asking forgiveness of all he harmed in that and every lifetime. He is asking that you, Gerri and Rory, act as surrogates for all who have been injured by him. This forgiveness will free Daniel and all who have been connected at a soul level to the pain he caused."

Rory and Gerri listened as Pam repeated Shadow's words. Then Pam watched them look at each other and move over to the image of Lucas. They each took one of his hands.

Rory spoke silently, "On behalf of all connected to you, I forgive you of all hurts, real or imagined, of all unkempt promises, real or imagined, that we and all others have suffered at your hands in this or any lifetime."

Gerri gently removed energy cords that covered Lucas, cords that represented injuries, anger, blame, and guilt. These were cords that had tied him to others, and they to him, keeping all of them locked into harmful patterns.

As these energy cords were removed, Pam turned them over to the angels with Divine love and the cords were transformed instantly to the white Light of Love. When she had completed the task, Rory removed the energy cords connected to themselves. Pam activated the Matrix on the release.

In the etheric realm, Lucas, Rory, and Gerri held each other. Tears of love and relief spilled from their eyes.

She asked the spiritual healers to bring this new adjustment into the energy fields and systems of Danny's physical body.

Pam stroked Daniel's hand as she opened her eyes. Her heart swelled with gratitude for the path she had chosen that allowed her to be a part of such incredible moments. Her early years of pain, the abuse that forced her to seek Shadow, and her ability to ask questions to bring answers for healing had all been worth the pain for the joy of this moment.

She leaned back and hummed a lullaby into the gathering dusk of the day.

CHAPTER 45

Gerri woke with a start.

The edges of her dream lingered. She closed her eyes. She reached gently into her mind to tug them back into place. The more she relaxed, the more vividly the dream pictures returned. Staying in that half-awake, half-asleep place, she memorized the frames.

There was Danny, but talking from an adult body.

"I'm okay," he was saying. "There's work that I'm doing in what looks like a coma. Don't worry. I love you. Remember your ability to see and hear. I will need your sensitivity to bring me through."

Then he began to fade and there was a glimpse of Dean, a sad Dean. It was only a glimpse, and like a ghost, he was gone. What did it mean? She would have to remember this so she could tell Rory. She searched the quiet for more pictures, more words, but there were none.

Gerri got up and found her journal. She quickly jotted down the dream, or was it a dream? Then she looked at the clock, it was 6 p.m. Rory should be home any time. She picked up the phone and called the hospital and asked for Danny's room.

"Hi, Pam. How is Danny?"

"He's about the same. How are you feeling?"

"I didn't think I would be able to rest, but I've been asleep for hours. Rory will be home soon and then I'll come to the hospital for the night," Gerri paused.

"And Pam," Gerri said.

"Yes," answered Pam.

"Danny is going to be okay."

Pam felt a catch in her throat. "Yes, sweetheart. I know he is. See you when you get here."

CHAPTER 46

Rory was glad for the busy schedule he had this morning. Too much time to think about Danny was not helpful. His heartache grabbed him at unsuspecting moments and submerged him. This was the fifth day of their vigil. He knew that Pam was at the hospital today and Gerri would be spending the night.

Joanne, his receptionist, was at his door. "Rory, Mr. Chase just called. He's too sick to keep his appointment." She spoke as she walked into his office. "That gives you a little over an hour before Mrs. Clark comes at four o'clock. She's your last appointment."

She had a cup of fresh coffee for him in her hands and placed it on the table next to his couch.

"Is there anything more you need?" Joanne asked. She had been extra watchful of his needs since Danny had been admitted to the hospital.

"No, I'm just fine. I'll just catch up on some of my notes for the files until Mrs. Clark comes," was his reply. "Any word from the hospital?"

"No," Joanne answered. "I'll let you know right away if they call."

Rory knew that she would. He had not really needed to ask the question, but he had been reassured with the asking.

Joanne closed the door softly as she left and Rory moved over to the couch with his file folders and pen. Setting them down, he took a sip of coffee and breathed deeply. Something inside of him, some tightly held sense of composure dropped away, and he found himself sobbing. He was a damn good therapist, a committed husband and father, well-respected in his community, and at this moment he felt like the biggest imposter in the world. He put the cup on the table and held his head in his hands. All the strength, the assurance drained out of him, and there, creeping out from its hidden place was his old self-doubt. Why did he think he could help people change? Who said he had answers? What good did it do to give your heart when behind the heart is someone others don't know. There were the old beliefs that he was not good enough, someone not worth listening too. How could he even think of helping Danny when there were others he had not been able to reach?

Instead of bringing his rational mind into the argument, he just let the emotions take him where they would. He hardly recognized the person he was telling himself he was and yet the words, the feelings were familiar. He had thought they were gone.

Finally, Rory asked who was there with so much pain. Like going into a dream he was three again. His baby brother, just home from the hospital, throwing up, throwing up, throwing up.

Fear on his mother's face. Parents struggling. Stress, worry, death hung over the little family. Rory, only three, tried to get their attention, struggled to be heard. Sibling jealousy, they said and medicated him.

He refused to go into the baby's room. Angry, misbehaving, jealous they labeled.

Rory could see himself as that tiny boy, his mind so sharp, his heart so heavy. Alone.

What is this about? Rory wondered. Why this memory, now? But the memory would not let go. Follow it, was all he heard.

I can't go into his room. Angry? Jealous? Doesn't fit. I know I love him. My brother is sick and I can't go into his room. I'll force myself to go down the hall towards his room.

"No," cried little Rory, "No! It hurts too much."

Surprised, the grown-up Rory asked, "Why? Why does it hurt?"

Little Rory sobbed, "Because I know. I know what he needs to make him better. They won't listen. They won't listen. They won't listen."

Sobs erupted and overcame Rory. His tears were soul deep. Stacy at Glacier Park, clients still in pain. Three year old Rory sobbed. Three, he knew the answer and no one would listen. Rory wept.

"I knew all the time, but they wouldn't listen. I was too little. I was trying to tell them." Rory remembered in wonder. "They couldn't hear me."

His ways to get their attention were labeled jealousy and anger. He was given drugs. Remembering, Rory sobbed. Such deep sorrow, the pain so intense. Even now, in memory, this little boy could not be near his baby brother.

All these years Rory had bought their words; he had been acting out, he was troublesome, disruptive. Rory's old thinking surfaced, "I am not heard. I think I know, but I don't really. Others know better than I do. I'll be quiet. I must be wrong. Just let others work it out. My ideas are not good ones. Who am I to think I can stop pain?" Judgments he had struggled with his whole life flooded him.

He became aware of how this intensity of pain at age three had burned into his soul. The commitment to help others, the strength that it took to overcome his own inner objections, and even suggestions from others that he not try so hard had roots in his three-year-old self. Rory began to understand.

He saw. Young children know. They have alert, intelligent minds. He had bought the wrong concepts! He wondered about Daniel. Did he know?

Rory reached out to himself as the young three year old with greater respect.

Here on his office couch, in his imagination, Rory returned to the world where he was still three and in great pain.

"Little Rory," he said to the young boy. "I know that you know what to do, but your parents have to do it their way. Perhaps you can go into your brother's room and explain that to him. You could let him know that even though you know what to do; they have to figure some things out for themselves. Would you like to do that?"

"Yes," was little Rory's response, relieved that someone had heard and understood.

Rory focused and watched the little boy move down the hall and open the door. Psychically, he stood at the door as little Rory went in and stood by the crib where his baby brother lay.

"You can tell him that you know what to do to help him," suggested Rory, the man.

Silence.

Little Rory spoke. "I told him."

Silence.

"Does he understand?" asked Rory, the man.

"Yes."

And then another pause.

"He knows what to do too," was the reply.

Rory was stunned. His little brother knew. As he suffered, he knew. Both of those young boys knew what to do to heal the problem, their knowing locked inside with no words to speak. What else might children know that adults will not hear? The old memory softened, the two boys hugged, and a peace filled them. They turned to look at Rory. He gave them a thumbs up and blew them a kiss.

"We made it through just fine," he said. The boys laughed, their pain gone.

Rory was a vigorous man, with several degrees, a brilliant mind. In his professional life, he was successful, innovative. He had an unwavering commitment to his clients. Now, from some deep place inside, a new door opened. He knew he could acknowledge that he did know. Rory stood and spoke what he had been afraid to say. Powerful words, solid, commanding, that would not be silent or allow objection.

"My son knows what he is doing and what is needed. The past must be changed for the present to change, and I hold the space for him to know and for me to hear."

And in that moment a dream floated through an open window. Driva, his ruthless father from the past, was with him in the room. "You were right when you were my son. You did know a better way. My cruelty was intentional and I was wrong. I want you to know that I am sorry. Will you forgive me?" he asked.

"With all of my heart," was Rory's reply. With that, Driva's face flickered, became a sleepy Danny, and then faded.

CHAPTER 47

Off and on while Danny slept, Gerri practiced listening. She closed her eyes, relaxed her mind, and told Danny she was there to hear what he needed. Sometimes she heard nothing and other times she heard a word or two.

"Thanks, mom." or "We're here."

Nothing momentous occurred, no miracles or flashes of insight. But Gerri trusted and remained available. Toward morning, Gerri heard a slight cry from Danny. Instantly she opened her eyes. Suddenly, a monitoring alarm went off and Danny's nurse rushed into the room.

Panic and fear gripped Gerri's body.

Clear as anything she had ever heard came the words, "Now is the time, Mom. This looks like a crisis, but it's only a message giver. I need you to get the message."

Gerri quickly went to Danny's bed, laid her hands on his tiny body, and commanded that his healers and angels bless and stabilize his physical world. Then kissing his forehead, she left the room. She went immediately to the quiet of the hospital chapel and stilled her mind.

"Who within Danny's world and energy fields knows the reason for this crisis?" she asked. Then, as she tried to move herself psychically to her son, she sensed a huge barrier, one that seemed impenetrable. With her mind she searched all around the form for a way through but could find no opening. She breathed and pulled her mind back in order to sense it more clearly. It was a large barrier around Danny, a barrier that she needed to get through. She asked what she was seeing and waited for the answer.

"This is a webbing of parasites, their devices, and residue," came her answer from Katumee, her guide. "It is like Danny is in a nest of vipers who are determined to own him and his energy."

Gerri was appalled and anxious. "What can I do?" she asked with an open heart.

"Remember the work that Pam has done. We are here to tell you that as a female and Daniel's mother, you have the right to keep his space clear of all energies that are not for his highest good, are not of the Divine Family. All you have to do is stand firm in the face of this intense nest. Say, "You are not of my son's light. You are parasites here. You have no right to be in his space or on our planet. I command that you be removed back to your home.""

Gerri focused on the energy barrier and did as she had been told, commanding as only a mother could.

"Now," said Katumee, "send a flow of sacred energy into the center of their nest, their grip will be released and his healing can be completed."

Gerri felt her maternal heart pull the strength and command from the depth of her being. She imagined lazar energy of Sacred Light shot into the center of this mass. She made a psychic command, "I demand the removal of all energy not of our Divine Light and residue be removed back to its beginning." She held that command. Gradually, like a mist, the barrier and nest dissipated, thinned, and evaporated. In what seemed like only minutes, the writhing energy was totally gone.

When she felt the space was clear, she asked again, "Who within Danny's world and body knows the reason for this crisis? What allowed these vipers?"

"I do," the answer came into her mind. The voice was vicious, menacing. "I bargained with Lucas. He gave me permission. I have a right to reside in his heart!"

As Gerri dialogued with this energy, she heard the story.

"What is your intention?" she asked.

"What it has always been," The voice spit out. "To stop him from living and experiencing love. Love isn't for my world. Love loosens my control. Life on this planet must be lived from control and manipulation or not at all. I will stop his heart if he reaches out to love."

Gerri called in her angels. Working from the authority of a female, of a mother, she commanded the removal of the parasitic devise anchored in Danny's heart. When that was done, she asked the healers to correct any damage in his heart, and circuitry systems. As she worked she was more than a mom. She was a healer detached from the gravity of the situation and totally connected to the stability of Divine Love.

"Are there any other messages for us to get at this time in order for Danny to be healthy?" she asked.

"Yes. Because of a contract you made with Danny before this lifetime, there needs to be a commitment from you to your path of intuition and inner knowing," replied her guide, Katumee.

"That I gratefully give," was her reply.

"Then there is nothing more at this time."

Gerri breathed and the emotional impact hit her. She cried as she rushed back to Danny's room. The nurse met her by the door.

"He's doing fine-there was a little scare, but he settled right down. His heart appeared to stop, but then it fluttered and his heartbeat has been strong and regular. We will be watching him very closely," the nurse assured Gerri.

"The doctor ordered some medication to use if we need it, but we haven't given him any," the nurse informed Gerri. Then she looked into the young mom's eyes. "Are you okay?"

"Yes, yes, I'm fine." Gerri wiped her eyes. "I just need to call my husband.

"Thank you so much for helping us with Danny. We've needed you to get through this with him. Thank you!" And Gerri went into Danny's room to sit by her first-born and affirm her commitment and love.

Within the week, Rory and Gerri were carrying Danny out of the hospital. Gerri's parents, along with Pam and Bob, waited for them at home. Everyone so relieved to have this ordeal behind them.

Rory and Gerri had been cautioned to watch Danny carefully for any signs of brain impairment and were to bring him often for check-ups. But, in Gerri's heart, she knew that the momentous event was over. Everyone had done their part well!

CHAPTER **48**

Those who had decided to be part of the children's project group were meeting to share their successes, new ideas, and to plan the next step. Their questions were always: "Will our techniques make the changes we want? If not, what will?"

Everyone was excited as they arrived. They knew of Danny's brush with death and were overjoyed that he was home and well. Rory greeted them as they came to the door and ushered them into the living room.

As soon as Rory opened the meeting to feedback from those who had had sessions with children since the last time they met, Jack Cooper, the astrologer, cleared his throat. "I want to share what happened for a 16 year old I was asked to work with. He has had such a devastating time in school. I've been in this business of reading planetary influences for a long time, so what I heard from his parents was not new. Anyway, he was struggling to stay in school and had really been frustrated for quite some time. I talked with him about what his astrology chart said about him.

"I explained that I was viewing the planets as they were in the sky at the moment of his birth. Some call it an energy snapshot at his birth. Anyway, some new ideas opened for him. He has a lot of spiritual gifts. Since those gifts are not acknowledged in our society, he has not been helped to acknowledge them. They give him a sense of fantasy and unreality, and could lead to drug use. I explained that he hadn't planned to use these energies to go with the drug scene. Doing drugs would be a sign that he hadn't found his place. I suggested that he use his imagination to ask for a spiritual teacher. With his gifts, he would have a unique way of thinking, an artistic bent, storytelling ability, etc. which could be very valuable to him. I told him that I suspect that he feels at home with unique ideas. He has a very active mind, is not a traditional thinker. Therefore, school seems unfulfilling to him. I suggested he not be afraid to think differently, and that he should be careful not to get trapped in fear thinking. I suggested that he go to the library, and begin checking out books with different philosophies or biographies. Start looking to understand his way of viewing the world.

"He got very excited and his parents have reported that he is happier. We're not home free yet, but it is a good step," Jack smiled as he sat down. "I guess one of the reasons I stay in this field because this kind of feedback is so consistent."

He then turned to Pam and asked, "What happened when you worked with him?"

"Well," responded Pam, "He and I had a session. I think he was a bit hesitant about this new approach, but he was a real trooper, willing to try.

"He had mentioned that his feet were always cold and told me, as you've mentioned, that school was very difficult for him. As I scanned his body, it was clear that he had pulled his energy into such a tight ball that there was very little of it flowing to sustain his body. It was like he was living in one room and the rest of his house was empty with no heat. I also found an old configuration. Whether he had lived a lifetime as a female or had taken this belief from a female in his genetic family does not really matter. It came from a lifetime when he or the ancestor had been labeled a witch and had been tortured for simply using intuitive gifts. The beliefs that resulted were, 'I am powerless, just give up,' and 'angry men are dangerous.'

"The pattern is that when he is around men, and especially males who act as if they are authorities, his automatic response is to feel stress and become powerless. A perfect foundation for attracting bullies, which he has.

"I did TAG work to transform the energy of that old lifetime and harmonize the flow within his present systems. His feet were warm when he got up from the table and he e-mailed me to say that he finds himself feeling less reactive in situations where before he had felt bullied."

Pam looked over at Jack and concluded, "I agree that there is still more that our group can give him, but I am very excited and so are his parents,"

Evelyn stood up. "I want to report on a project that Pam and I have been designing. It has to do with the Indigo children. We have evaluated young Sara as well as John. I know that we have a long way to go because it's new territory, but I wanted to let you know what we are finding.

"I made copies of the initial evaluation. You can see we are using some work that was done by others. Since this is such a new concept, few have forged ahead with it yet, but we feel that it's critical that information be gathered and disseminated.

"On page one there is a table with seven types of abilities listed. The work to find tests that reveal more than the memorization skill that standard IQ tests indicate was done by a man in the Mid-West. He felt that our school systems were losing too many students because they measured only memorization ability. A student's creativity, leadership, dexterity, etc., valuable abilities were ignored. We've included an identification chart to evaluate a child according to these seven innate skills."

Evelyn looked around and then continued.

"Then, Pam has come up with a battery of questions about a child's spiritual plans, negative patterns, genetic or other life carryover, and the soul's purpose for this life. We have found that the parents are very pleased with the information because it has given them a basis to understand their child.

"I'd like to work with this Indigo portion of the project. It is exciting to me and I know it will make a positive impact for children. That is what I am looking for."

As the group shared their experiences and the change in relationships because of the work with the children, Rory smiled. Then he stood up to share. All eyes were on him.

"As all of you know, Gerri and I had our own dark night of the soul with our son Danny. We want to thank you for the calls, prayers, and concern. He's home now, sleeping in his own crib, and there seems to be no sign of any problems. But, we are watching him pretty closely."

He cleared his throat and ran his fingers through his blond hair.

"I don't want to assume that we need extreme situations in order to grow and deepen, but I want to tell you that these past weeks have forced me to evaluate my priorities and have taken me into parts of myself that I didn't know still existed. And through it all, I am a changed man, thankful for the process. I know we're on the right track. I also know that our work may not always be easy or popular, but from personal experience, I know it will change lives. Others may not hear us, but we hear, we know and most importantly, the children will know!" he said emphatically.

"It isn't about learning from the past, it's about really letting go of the past. Only in a truly empty space can we create a new world for our children. And so I am giving warning: all of you have patterns, fears, or doubts hidden away. They will surface and when they do, reach out to the group. We must be willing to help each other eliminate our negative patterns. We expect new lives for the children and unless we release the patterns and pain that we are holding, it will not happen. We have been looking for the answer and it is us."

"We need mature, healthy adults before the children will be free. Thanks for being such amazing people." With that he sat down, his clarity affecting everyone in the group.

CHAPTER 49

Gerri and Pam were sharing a quiet morning over steaming mugs of coffee. Danny was sleeping safely in his crib. This was the first chance that the two had to compare notes since Danny's return home. After asking lots of questions of Shadow and her team, Pam wanted to visit with Gerri.

"I know that I do not have the entire story yet," she was saying, "but the thing that I wanted to get feedback on is this female, male information. If what I am hearing is correct, it puts an entirely new spin of the need for women to have choice in their lives."

"I am getting very similar guidance," replied Gerri. "In fact, Danny's last major crisis in the hospital required that I clear him and his space. There were some really nasty energy forms. I was told that because I was a female, I had the authority and responsibility to do the clearing. Does that make sense to you?"

"Yes! This is how I understand it so far. The woman's womb is symbolic of the space holder that she is. These incredibly parasitic forms from outside of our greater family have plastered themselves throughout our energy fields. They virtually have owned humanity and use fear energy in order to survive and to control. They can masquerade in human body suits or remain as energy forms whose powerful whispers cause actions. These outsiders are committed to fear in any form: conflict, injury, anything that increases mistrust among our greater family. Their nature and agenda is control, power, cruelty and that agenda leads to greater and greater death among humanity. Our pain and death is of no concern to them for we are not of their family. We are captive, the rats in their laboratory.

"Those souls from our Divine family who come into female bodies have the assignment to command the removal of these outsiders. You see, womb space as we normally think of it for gestation and birthing, is only a model for the womb space of home, the womb space of schools, the womb space of nature, the womb space of the world's communities. We, as women, have been given the charge to decide what comes into the wombs and what nurtures healthy growth for those born onto the planet. We are the ones to set boundaries for all space, beginning with our womb. Women are to discern what will expand and what will constrict our loved ones and demand spaces that allow expansion. The truth is that females were to keep our world cleared of all that would bring fear and death. It is that Yin energy of leadership and wisdom that the world is crying for."

Gerri laughed, "Just a minor role in the scheme of things."

"Yes," Pam smiled, "and it is the Divine responsibility of the male to hold spiritual connection, heart connection and to nurture that female until the initial mission and clearing is complete."

As Gerri and Pam worked together with this new concept as womb holders, Gerri's sensitivity increased. In keeping her promise to Danny she was becoming more powerful and thereby more helpful in the work with the children.

CHAPTER 50

Word was beginning to spread. Parents were contacting Rory, Pam, or one of the other project members. Two adults had called Pam, especially anxious. They had made an appointment with her, asking if they could bring their nephew. He was the cause of their concern. Gerri had agreed to stay with the nephew, so she was at Pam's office when the family arrived. She watched the adults walking up the path toward the office with a tow-headed boy moving reluctantly in front of them. He's about 8 or 9, Gerri thought. The clients opened the front door and came into the office. Pam went forward to meet them and introduce herself.

Turning to Pam, the young man spoke, "This is my wife, Georgina. I am Ben and this young man is Bryan. Bryan is my wife's sister's son. My wife and I have been out of the country for several years and just got back a month ago. Bryan's parents are on a short business trip and asked us to take care of him for them."

"Yes," interjected Georgina, "we are all struggling a bit getting to know each other and missing Bryan's mom and dad like heck."

"I'm Pam Hatcher and this is Gerri," Pam said to the adults.

Turning to the young boy, she invited, "Bryan, Gerri can play with you while I visit with your aunt and uncle. There are lots of books and there are toys in the backyard."

Facing Ben and Georgina she continued, "We can have some private time without Bryan becoming too bored," she assured her clients.

"We really appreciate this," the man spoke.

Then Georgina turned to Bryan, "We'll be about forty-five minutes with Mrs. Hatcher. Can you go take your books and go play with Gerri? We won't be very far away."

Pam took the adults into her conference room. Gerri smiled at Bryan and reached for his hand. "Let's go see what we can find out in the backyard," she said.

Usually children took to Gerri very easily, but Bryan examined her with veiled, suspicious eyes, pushed her hand away, and followed her to the yard.

An hour later the meeting was over. Pam and Gerri sat to talk.

Gerri spoke up unable to contain her emotions.

"Remember what I told you about Danny and the inner dark energy I saw during the time that his heart was struggling? It was like a nest of writhing vipers?" Gerri's face showed the distaste as she spoke of that experience to Pam.

"Yes," replied Pam. "That nest of vipers who were determined to keep him and his energy as theirs. Those are the energies that we know as outsiders."

"Yes, well I had the same feeling about Bryan, only stronger. I don't know exactly what has happened to him, but it's not just the things we've talked about in our project meetings. This child has had something intentionally done to him and I feel danger and cruelty all around him."

"I can tell you, Gerri, that something is very wrong. Whatever is going on has Ben and Georgina very worried and Bryan's parents may somehow be a part of the problem." Pam looked somber.

"You know, it took all of my effort to just be with him. The hair on the back of my neck was standing on end! It was very creepy. I was asking for the healers to TAG and Transform constantly." Gerri sat by her friend.

Shadow and the TAG team watched quietly. They knew that these two women had what it took to help Bryan, this little tow-headed boy, and to blast open the dark worlds of secrets that most never see.

CHAPTER 51

"What do you think?" Pam whispered to Danielle. "Are you happy with your choice to stick around and help with the babies and the children?"

She shifted a focus in her head like changing to another radio station.

"Can't you feel my joy? This is just beginning and I am so jazzed!" came a reply typical of this new aspect of Pam's personality.